Praise for
JESSICA HART:

About A BRIDE FOR BARRA CREEK

"Jessica Hart pens a gripping tale...."
—*Romantic Times*

About TEMPORARY ENGAGEMENT

"Jessica Hart creates...characters who energize the
plot and keep you laughing out loud."
—*Romantic Times*

About KISSING SANTA

"Jessica Hart delivers delightful reading...."
—*Romantic Times*

Harlequin Romance® is thrilled to present a lively new
trilogy from JESSICA HART

City Brides

They're on the career ladder,
but just one step away from the altar!

Meet Phoebe, Kate and Bella...

When their best friend gets married,
these friends suddenly realize that they're fast approaching
thirty and haven't yet found Mr. Right—or even Mr. Maybe!

Living together in the center of London is a lot of fun,
but they refuse to admit that they spend more time
gossiping and groaning about the lack of eligible men
than actually looking for one....

But that's about to change.
If fate won't lend a hand, they'll make their own luck.
Whether it's a hired date or an engagement of convenience,
they're determined that the next wedding invitation they see
will be one of their own!

Look out for Kate's and Bella's stories:

August—*The Blind-Date Proposal* (#3761)
September—*The Whirlwind Engagement* (#3765)

FIANCÉ WANTED FAST!

Jessica Hart

City Brides

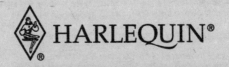

TORONTO • NEW YORK • LONDON
AMSTERDAM • PARIS • SYDNEY • HAMBURG
STOCKHOLM • ATHENS • TOKYO • MILAN • MADRID
PRAGUE • WARSAW • BUDAPEST • AUCKLAND

ISBN 0-373-03757-0

FIANCÉ WANTED FAST!

First North American Publication 2003.

Copyright © 2003 by Jessica Hart.

This edition published by arrangement with Harlequin Books S.A.

® and TM are trademarks of the publisher. Trademarks indicated with
® are registered in the United States Patent and Trademark Office, the
Canadian Trade Marks Office and in other countries.

Visit us at www.eHarlequin.com

Printed in U.S.A.

CHAPTER ONE

'MALLORY left you?' Josh lowered his water bottle and stared at Gib in surprise.

'Ironic, isn't it?' said Gib with a somewhat crooked grin, shifting his back against the ice wall and putting on his jacket. It had been hot work climbing the last pitch, but at this altitude you soon lost heat. 'The boot's usually on the other foot!'

Josh grimaced. 'I'm sorry to hear that,' he said slowly. 'I always liked Mallory. You seemed really good together too.'

'That's what I thought,' said Gib wryly. 'Mallory's a very special lady. Smart as anything and beautiful and independent...I really thought she was going to be different.'

He tapped the side of his crampons with his ice pick to loosen the balled ice. 'But then the old C word started cropping up and I knew that was the beginning of the end.'

'The what word?' asked Josh, diverted.

'Commitment.' Gib stared morosely out at the spectacular view.

They had stopped for a rest on a frozen ledge, high up on the mountain. It was still some way to the summit, but you could look out at the hills stretching off to the hazy horizon. Gib loved the mountains. The air was clean and pure and the only sound was the wind cutting icily through the brilliant sunlight.

He was glad that Josh had called him up and suggested a climb. It was good to be up here where everything was simple and there was not a tearful woman in sight.

It certainly made a nice change.

'Why are women so obsessed with commitment?' he demanded. 'They all start off pretending that they're independent and just want a good time, but you're lucky if you get to a third date without them planning their wedding dresses!'

'You and Mallory had been together a bit longer than three dates,' Josh pointed out reasonably. 'It's nearly a year now, isn't it?'

'Exactly!' grumbled Gib. 'We were getting along great, everything was fine...why did she have to go and spoil it?'

'What did she say?'

'Apparently I am completely unable to "commit" or to "relate".' Gib hooked his fingers in the air to add sarcastic emphasis to the inverted commas. 'According to Mallory, I just thought of her as part of some kind of smorgasbord of women!'

Josh looked blank. 'A smorgasbord?'

'You know, one of those buffet affairs where all the dishes are set out along a big table and you go round to help yourself to whatever you fancy.'

'Right,' said Josh, none the wiser.

'Mallory's theory is that I treat women like so many different dishes, so that even if I find one I really like, I won't be content to stick with one because I'll always be wondering if there might not be one I might like even better further along the table.' Gib gave an exclamation of disgust. 'Don't you hate it when women analyse you?'

Josh didn't answer directly. Behind the dark glasses that protected his eyes from the glare, his expression was unreadable as he studied the view and considered Mallory's theory.

'She's right, though, isn't she?' he said at last.

'Listen, whose side are you on?' demanded Gib.

'You're the one who said that she's a smart lady.'

'I just happen to like women,' said Gib defensively. 'What's wrong with that?'

'Nothing.'

'And women like me.' He scowled. 'I love women! It's ridiculous to say that I can't relate to them properly!'

'Is that what Mallory says?'

'She says I've got no idea how to be friends with a woman.' Gib sounded outraged. 'Can you believe that?'

'Yes.'

'What do you mean?' he asked, taken aback by the typically quiet, uncompromising reply. Josh was so...so...so *British*...sometimes!

Josh was checking the ropes. 'Have you ever had a platonic relationship with a woman? A good one?'

'Sure.'

'When?'

'When? Well, let's see...when...when...' Gib searched his mind frantically. 'OK, I can't think of anyone right this moment,' he was forced to acknowledge, 'but I'm sure there must have been someone. I bet you can't think of anyone either,' he added, going on the offensive.

It didn't faze Josh. 'Yes I can,' he said calmly. 'Bella is one of my best friends, probably the best friend I've got, in fact. We were students together, and we've been close ever since.'

'And you've never slept with her?'

'No.'

'I bet you wanted to!'

Josh shook his head. 'No, that would spoil our friendship. Bella's always got some man in tow, and I have girlfriends, but it's different with her. I prefer what we've got. I can talk to Bella in a way I can't talk to anyone else. We understand each other.

'It's nothing to do with sex,' he went on. 'You could never be friends with a woman in the same way.'

'Want a bet?' said Gib, ruffled.

'OK.'

'OK?'

Josh tied off the end of the rope and sat back against the rock. 'I'll bet you…let's say ten thousand dollars?…to the charity of your choice that you can't be friends with a woman.'

Gib laughed. 'Ten *thousand* dollars? You're kidding, right?'

'You can afford it.'

'Yeah, but can you?'

'I don't think I will have to,' said Josh with annoying calm.

Well, Gib wasn't a man who could turn down a challenge like that! His eyes narrowed.

'Being friends is a bit subjective, isn't it? How would we decide if I'd succeeded or not?'

Josh unwrapped an energy bar and chewed meditatively for a while. 'How would you feel about spending a few weeks in London?' he asked at last.

'It wouldn't be a problem, I guess,' said Gib, a bit thrown by the apparent *non sequitur*. 'It's easy enough to keep in touch with what's happening here wherever I am.'

Absently he took the bar Josh handed him out of his ruck-sack. 'As a matter of fact,' he went on slowly, 'it might suit me quite well. I've been thinking about developing more European connections and with this whole Mallory thing, I wouldn't mind leaving the country for a while. I could do without all those scenes about who takes what!'

'OK.' Josh nodded briskly. 'Here's the deal. Bella shares a house in south London with three other girls, but one of them is getting married soon, so they're going to have a spare room. I reckon I could arrange it for you to live with them for a while.' He grinned. 'I think it would be a real test for you! If at the end of six weeks Bella and Kate and Phoebe all describe you to me as a real friend, you name the charity and I'll send the cheque!'

'Hhmmnn.' Gib looked a bit dubious. 'What are these girls like?'

'They're just three very nice, very ordinary English girls.'

'And that's it? I just live with them for six weeks and be their friend?'

'There's one more condition,' said Josh. 'You have to go incognito. You've had too many attractive, successful women falling over themselves for you here. Mallory's a psychologist and before that there was the TV presenter and that model...what was her name? The one with the legs up to her armpits?'

'Verona?'

'That's the one.' Josh allowed himself to remember her legs for a moment. They really had been spectacular.

'Anyway, the point is, you're spoilt!' he went on. 'It'll be different in London. The girls won't know anything about you, so you won't be able to buy their affection or impress them the way you do here. You'll just have to be yourself and if you can't be friends with them under those circumstances then you'll just have to accept that Mallory is right!'

Gib's face was inscrutable behind the dark glasses that cut out the mountain glare as he studied the horizon.

He was thinking about his father, who was now on his fourth wife. Gib got on with his father fine, but he didn't want to be like him. He had seen too many women in tears because his father's idea of commitment turned out to be very different from theirs.

Gib, on the other hand, prided himself on never making

promises he couldn't fulfil. He always made it clear to girl-friends that he wasn't offering happy ever after, and frankly couldn't see what was so wrong with being honest about wanting to live in the present without tying yourself to a future you weren't ready for.

But that didn't mean he couldn't be friends with a woman! No way was Gib prepared to accept that his attitude was anything like his father's. If he didn't have a female friend like Josh, it was just because most of the women he knew were more interested in being wives than friends.

Well, he would show Josh and Mallory and his father that he was perfectly capable of building a relationship with a woman that was based on friendship rather than sex. He would take the bet.

'Ten thousand dollars?' he said.

'Ten thousand dollars.'

'And I get to choose the charity that gets the money?'

'Only if you win. Otherwise I do.'

'OK, then.' Gib grinned as he held out his hand to Josh. 'You're on!'

Phoebe collapsed onto the sofa, kicking off her shoes and swinging her legs up with a sigh of relief. 'My feet are killing me! Next time I go to a wedding, remind me not to wear stilettos!'

'They are fab, though,' said Bella, handing out mugs of tea. It had been a sad moment when they all realised that after drinking champagne all day tea was all they really wanted. 'Sometimes you just have to suffer for style.'

Kate took her tea gratefully. She was lolling on one of the deep chairs, with her legs dangling over one arm.

'Personally I'd be exhausted if I had to be that stylish all the time. I'd no idea it was going to be such a smart wed-ding. Did you *see* some of those women there? It must be a full-time job looking like that! I felt so dowdy, like I was one of those embarrassing relatives you have to invite but nobody wants to talk to.'

'I know,' Phoebe agreed gloomily. 'You could tell they weren't at all surprised that we couldn't muster a single boyfriend between us.'

'Oh, come on, it wasn't that bad,' said Bella. 'I thought it was excellent! I love smart weddings like that. If I ever get married, I'm going to do it like Caro—the posh church, reception at some classy club, hundreds of guests all looking incredibly stylish.'

'Better get some new friends then,' said Phoebe rather indistinctly through a mouthful of chocolate digestive. 'If you're going to impose a fashion code, half of us won't be able to come. Kate and Josh and I will be camped out on the church steps just to get a glimpse of you as you sweep by!'

Bella grinned. 'Oh, Josh brushes up pretty well, and I'm sure I'll be able to find a dark corner to put you two in!'

'Better tell your father to start saving now,' put in Kate. 'That wedding today must have cost a packet.'

'I think Anthony must have contributed. It's not as if he can't afford it!'

'Well, I'd rather have a traditional country wedding,' said Kate. 'Just family and good friends and a marquee in my parents' garden so we can walk back from the village church. I'm going to have my two little nieces as bridesmaids,' she went on dreamily. 'They'd look sweet in taffeta with puffed sleeves and—'

She stopped as she saw Phoebe and Bella looking at her. 'Not that I've given it much thought, of course,' she said, but had the grace to blush.

'Of course not!' said Bella. She turned to Phoebe who

was saying 'What about you, Phoebe? Would you go for urban chic or the perfect country wedding?'

Phoebe concentrated on brushing biscuit crumbs from her dress. 'Neither. I think the best option would be to run away and get married on the quiet so that you don't have to plan anything. At least that way you would know the bridegroom was going to turn up!'

'Sorry, Phoebe,' said Bella contritely. 'I forgot you'd already been through all this.'

Phoebe attempted a careless shrug. 'Oh, well, it's been over a year now.'

Sixteen months, three weeks and four days, in fact.

Not that she was counting.

'And we didn't really get as far as planning the wedding before Ben changed his mind.'

Kate and Bella preserved a tactful silence. They knew quite well that she and Ben had been childhood sweethearts and that the chances of her not having spent most of her life thinking about the day they would get married were remote to say the least.

At least her parents hadn't sent out any invitations. She had been spared the humiliation of returning presents and answering sympathetic notes, although everybody had known, of course.

Phoebe picked up her tea. 'Anyway,' she said, 'I don't think any of us need panic about planning our weddings just yet. It's not as if hordes of men are desperate to sweep us off to the altar!'

'No,' Bella and Kate sighed.

'I'm beginning to think there's something wrong with this house,' she went on gesturing with her mug around the kitchen where they were sitting. 'It's as if it's cursed with a special man-repelling aura! Do you think I should sell it?'

The other two sat up in alarm. 'No!'

'I like it here,' Kate insisted.

'So do I,' said Bella, adding more practically, 'and we'd never be able to afford anywhere nearly as nice to live.'

'I know what you mean about the aura, though,' Kate reassured Phoebe. She brightened. 'Maybe that explains why Seb has been so funny recently?

'I think we should try feng shui before you do anything drastic,' she hurried on before Phoebe could start on the other possibilities for Seb's defection. 'I've got a friend who does it. Apparently you can change your luck just by shifting your furniture around a bit and keeping the loo seat down so that bad spirits can't get into the house.'

'Well, that shouldn't be a problem with no blokes around,' observed Phoebe glumly.

'Kate's right,' said Bella. 'Well, not about the feng shui maybe, but about not selling. It's a lovely house, and I certainly don't want to move. I must admit it's not going to be the same without Caro, though,' she added. 'I can't believe she'd be selfish enough to leave us just to get married!'

'I know,' agreed Phoebe. 'I mean, what's in it for her?' She gestured expansively with her free hand around the kitchen which was in its usual state of shabby chaos.

'Why would she want to leave all this for a big house in Fulham, a cleaner and an adoring husband?'

'I can't imagine,' said Kate loyally. 'You wouldn't catch me doing anything like that! Maybe she'll miss us so much she'll come back?'

'I don't think we should count on it,' sighed Phoebe. 'I know it's going to be hard to replace her, but I'm afraid I'm going to have to find someone else for her room or I won't be able to pay the mortgage. Neither of you have heard of anyone who's looking for somewhere to live, have you?'

They shook their heads. 'Not anyone I would want to share with anyway,' amended Bella.

'It looks like I might have to advertise then.'

'I'm not sure that's a good idea,' said Kate nervously. 'We could get all sorts of weirdos. Remember that film where the new flatmate murders the first girl and takes over her life? We could get someone like that.'

'Or worse,' said Bella. 'We could get someone obsessed with country dancing.'

They were all silent for a moment, brooding on the thought.

'Or we might get someone obsessed with cleaning,' suggested Phoebe. She looked ruefully around the kitchen. 'That wouldn't be too bad. She'd have plenty to keep her busy, anyway.'

'I shared with a girl like that once.' Bella shuddered at the memory. 'She was completely neurotic about cleaning. There were Post-its all over the flat with instructions about taking out the rubbish or reminders about the dusting rota, and the moment you made yourself a mug of tea she would whip out a coaster and follow you around until you put it down.'

She grimaced. 'It was seriously spooky! I think we'd be better off with a serial killer or a country dancer.'

'I think I'd rather sell the house,' sighed Phoebe.

'What about that guy Josh was talking about?' asked Kate suddenly. 'Did he mention him to you, Phoebe?'

'Briefly.' Phoebe drained her mug. 'What did he say his name was again?'

Kate tipped her head back and contemplated the ceiling while she searched her erratic memory. 'Gus?'

'Gib,' Bella corrected her.

'That was it.' Phoebe remembered her conversation with Josh as she helped herself to another biscuit. 'Doesn't he only want somewhere temporary, though? We need to find someone permanent.'

'Yes, but if he was here for a while it would give us time to find someone we really like,' said Kate.

Phoebe munched doubtfully. 'We don't really know anything about him, though,' she pointed out.

'We know he's a friend of Josh's.'

'But why does he only want to be here for a few weeks?' she asked Bella, who as Josh's best friend could be presumed to know more than the rest of them.

'I'm not sure. Josh was a bit vague about that. I know he lives in California, but that's about all. I got the impression he might be in a bit of financial difficulty, which is why he wants somewhere relatively cheap.'

Phoebe looked dubious. 'If he's that short of cash, why fly all the way from the States to London?'

'Maybe he just wants to get away from home for a bit,' suggested Kate, brightening perceptively at the idea of someone else to take under her wing. 'Perhaps his heart has been broken, and he needs some time and space to lick his wounds?'

'Oh, yes, that's *so* likely!' said Phoebe, rolling her eyes. 'There you are in California, with all that sunshine and spectacular scenery, and you think, "I need to cheer myself up, what can I do? I know, I'll go and spend six weeks in Tooting!" I mean, nothing against Tooting—I know we like it—but you've to admit that a suburb in south-west London isn't top of everybody's top ten tourist destinations.'

'It doesn't matter why he's coming, does it?' said Bella practically. 'Josh wouldn't have recommended him if he hadn't been able to pay the rent, and he can't be too awful if he's a friend of his. Why not think about it, Phoebe? Quite apart from anything else, it would be fun to have a man around the house again!'

Kate sat up straighter. 'And maybe Seb will hear about it and be jealous,' she added hopefully.

Privately, Phoebe thought it extremely unlikely that Kate's on-off, but more usually off, boyfriend, known to the rest of the world as Slimy Seb, would care one way or the other, but she knew that Kate lived in daily hope of hearing from him again. She was the only person Phoebe knew who actually believed that if you kept kissing a frog you'd eventually end up with a prince.

'You never know,' she said, avoiding Bella's eye. 'All right then, we'll give this Gib a go!'

Gib's mouth pulled down at the corners as he looked up at his home for the next six weeks. It was part of a terrace of identically narrow, faintly shabby Victorian houses that lined the street, and in the dank drizzle of that April evening even the tub of flowering bulbs at the front door failed to relieve the atmosphere of gloom.

Gib couldn't help thinking about his home on the Pacific coast, with its huge, light, open rooms and its view of the ocean, and he sighed. He was beginning to wonder if he might regret taking up the challenge Josh had thrown him.

Behind him, the taxi driver cleared his throat meaningfully, and Gib stepped up to the door and pushed the bell, his most charming smile at the ready. A bet was a bet, and it was too late to change his mind now.

He hadn't heard the bell ring inside, and pushed it again just as the door jerked open and he found himself looking at a tall, slender girl with the fiercest green eyes he had ever seen. She had a swing of straight dark hair, straight dark brows and a generous mouth that belied the severity of her expression.

Gib's smile blinked off in surprise. Had he got the right address? He distinctly remembered Josh saying that all three girls were very ordinary. They're just nice, friendly girls, he had said.

This girl didn't look at all ordinary to Gib , and she didn't look very friendly either.

'Yes?' she snapped.

'I'm John Gibson.' Gib put his smile back on, but it bounced right off her. 'Gib to my friends. And you must be Phoebe, Bella or Kate?'

'I'm Phoebe,' she acknowledged reluctantly, and frowned. 'We weren't expecting you until tomorrow.'

'Tomorrow was the original plan, but I was all ready and an earlier flight came up, so I thought I might as well just come on over and turn up.'

He had the bluest eyes Phoebe had ever seen, and they danced in a way that instantly made her feel boring and repressed for not being the kind of spontaneous person that changed arrangements at a whim and breezed across the Atlantic with about as much fuss as she would make popping down to the shop on the corner.

Less, probably.

Phoebe had had a bad day. Her boss, Celia, had been in a vile mood, nitpicking and throwing tantrums with an even greater regularity than normal. Escaping at last, she had spent more than forty minutes waiting for a bus which turned out to be only going as far as Clapham Junction anyway. Too fed up to hang around in the rain, she had set off to walk the rest of the way, without thinking about the fact that it would take her nearly an hour and that she was carrying two heavy folders and wearing quite unsuitable shoes, and when she finally hobbled into the kitchen she had discovered that the pilot light on the boiler had gone out, so there was no hot water for a bath.

And now there was this Gib on her doorstep.

Sod's law, thought Phoebe morosely. Be at your best with your hair perfectly in place and your lipstick perfectly applied, and you could be sure that when the doorbell went unexpectedly it would be someone doing market surveys or that man who kept trying to get them to change their electricity supplier.

Look and feel like a limp rag, however, and you could guarantee that the most attractive man you had ever seen in the flesh would turn up on the doorstep!

When she looked at him properly, she could see that he wasn't actually that handsome—his features were too irregular for classic good looks—but he had a quirky, mobile face with eyes so blue and so alive that somehow that was all that you noticed.

Phoebe was distinctly unnerved by the sheer vibrancy of the man. He had that relaxed yet vivid air of someone who spent his life in the sun. Just looking at him was like getting a blast of ozone. He was the sort of man who ought by rights to be at the helm of a yacht or plunging into the ocean waves with a surfboard under his arm, not standing in this grey south London street evidently wondering why she was staring at him.

Recollecting herself, Phoebe stepped back and held open the door. 'You'd better come in,' she said awkwardly.

Gib stayed where he was on the doorstep. 'The thing is, I've got a bit of a problem,' he admitted, and turned to indicate the taxi which was waiting in the street with its meter ticking at a rate of knots.

'I lost my wallet somewhere between LA and the arrivals hall at Heathrow. I think someone might have lifted it in the baggage hall, but anyway it's gone. I reported it to the police and have cancelled all my cards but I thought the best thing I could do would just be to get a taxi here and hope someone was in.'

He looked back at Phoebe with a rueful smile that she was sure was perfectly calculated to have most females swooning at his feet. 'You wouldn't have some cash to pay the taxi driver, would you? I'll pay you back, of course, as soon as I've sorted something out.'

Phoebe forced herself to resist the smile. It was just a little too like Slimy Seb's, who only ever came round when he wanted something and who was always patting his pockets and discovering that he had 'forgotten' his wallet, knowing quite well what a soft touch Kate was.

This Gib looked as if he was out of the same mould, one of those cocky, charming types that thought all they had to do was smile and everyone else would fall over themselves to do whatever they wanted. Phoebe didn't trust men like that. She had met too many of them, and seen too many friends like Kate hurt by their selfish behaviour to ever succumb herself.

Gib was watching her expression and reading her lack of enthusiasm without difficulty. 'Hey, it's no problem,' he said. 'I'll just get the taxi to take me to Josh's office. I'm sure I'll find someone there to bail me out.'

It was lucky that he had mentioned Josh. As Bella's best friend, Josh spent a lot of time in the house, and Phoebe was very fond of him. If Josh vouched for Gib, she had better not leave him to sort out his own problems the way she was strongly tempted to do.

'There's no need for that.' She managed a brittle smile. 'I'll just go and get my purse.'

'Thanks, I really appreciate that,' said Gib as the taxi drove off. 'I'll let you have the money back tomorrow.'

That was what Seb always said to Kate, too.

'Everything's a bit of mess,' said Phoebe stiffly as she led the way to the kitchen at the back of the house. 'We were going to tidy up for you tonight.'

They had planned a special welcoming meal as well. Bella was doing the shopping on her way home, but of

course spontaneous types like Gib never thought of how
they might mess up anyone else's plans, did they?

'Hey, I didn't want anyone to go to any trouble,' said
Gib, alarmed by her frosty manner. 'Josh said you'd just
treat me like a friend and let me muck in with the rest of
you.'

'Now that you've turned up early, it looks like that's what
you're going to have to do,' said Phoebe, carrying the kettle
over to the sink to fill it.

Gib eyed her warily, picking up on the hostility but not
quite sure what he had done to provoke it. Maybe she was
cross like this with everyone, which would be a crying
shame with that warm, creamy skin and that lush mouth, he
thought and then remembered that he wasn't supposed to be
thinking like that. *All you've got to do is be a friend*, Josh
had said. What could be easier than that?

Clicking on the kettle, Phoebe turned to face him, and
Gib looked quickly away. 'Nice kitchen,' he said.

It was a big, cluttered room with fitted cupboards at one
end and at the other a shabby sofa and deep armchair covered with an ethnic-looking throw. In the middle was an
antique pine table submerged beneath a welter of half-read
newspapers, magazine cuttings, recipe books and files with
papers spilling out of them. Gib spotted an iron, a collection
of nail varnishes, a sequin bag, and—he did a double take—
yes, a huge tabby cat curled up in a nest of papers.

The kitchen run by his housekeeper at home had gleaming steel surfaces and was so intimidatingly tidy that Gib
rarely ventured in there. This room was messier and a lot
less hygienic, he thought, glancing at the cat, but infinitely
more inviting. The kind of room where you could sit down
with a bottle of wine and relax without worrying about what
anyone else was thinking of you.

'It's the warmest room in the house,' said Phoebe, looking around and trying to see it through his eyes. 'We spend all our time in here, as you can probably tell.'

'Whose is the cat?'

'Kate's.' Phoebe regarded it without affection. 'She's got the softest heart in the world. She's always coming back with these poor bedraggled creatures she's rescued, and then we all have to run around finding homes for them, but no one will take that cat, worse luck. Anyway, it probably wouldn't go,' she sighed. 'It's much too comfortable here. Kate spoils it, and Bella and I are terrified of it. Which reminds me,' she added, 'be careful when you come down in the mornings. It bites your ankles until you feed it!'

Josh hadn't mentioned savage cats when he made his bet, Gib thought a little sourly. He hadn't mentioned Phoebe's frosty manner either. Gib just hoped that there weren't any other nasty surprises in store for him.

As if understanding that they were talking about it, the cat got to its feet and stretched. Seeing the size of it, and the ferocious-looking teeth, Gib gave it a wide berth, but it only gave him a contemptuous stare and jumped off the table to land with a thud on the kitchen floor.

Phoebe watched it stalk out of the room and for the first time ever she warmed to it. Here at least was one other creature unlikely to be impressed by Gib's smile and spontaneity. Kate and Bella were bound to fall for his charm, but Gib would find that she and the cat were made of sterner stuff!

CHAPTER TWO

PHOEBE had been pouring boiling water into a teapot, and now got out a couple of mugs. 'Kate and Bella will be back later,' she said. 'Would you like some tea?'

'Great,' he said with the suggestion of a smile. 'Now I know I'm back in England!'

'How long have you been away?'

Gib thought a bit. 'Nearly eighteen years now.'

'That's a long time,' said Phoebe, trying to calculate how old that made him. It was difficult to tell just by looking at him. He had the solidity of an older man, and there were definite creases around the edges of his eyes. He had to be in his late thirties at least, but he had a disconcerting mixture of dynamism and lazy good humour that seemed to belong to someone much younger.

She wished Kate or Bella would come home. Something about him made her feel tongue-tied and awkward and—worse—boring. It was a feeling that reminded her all too painfully of that terrible time when she had wept as she had asked Ben 'why?', and he had told her that Lisa was sweet and feminine and fun.

Not like her.

Gib was obviously fun, too.

'What do you do?' she asked stiltedly. Too bad if he thought it was a boring question. She was just being polite. That was what boring people did.

Gib didn't roll his eyes at the banality of her conversation, but he wasn't very forthcoming either. 'Oh, this and that,' he said vaguely as he picked up his mug.

Silence didn't seem to bother him at all. Phoebe stirred her tea unnecessarily and sought for something else to say. 'Are you going to be working while you're here?' she managed eventually.

'I'm looking into setting up a couple of projects.'

It all sounded a bit vague to Phoebe, but if he wanted her to think he had a flourishing business with projects on the go, let him. She knew how sensitive men were about their success or lack of it, and she wasn't that interested anyway.

Gib was looking around him with interest, apparently unconcerned by her awkward attempts to make conversation. Phoebe couldn't get over how blue his eyes were, and she studied him surreptitiously, wondering if he wore contact lenses to make them that colour, only to flush with annoyance when he caught her looking at him and smiled.

Phoebe jerked her gaze away. He obviously thought she couldn't keep her eyes off him. How smug could you get? Really, he was just like Seb.

Typical, she thought glumly. The one attractive man to swim into her orbit since Ben, and he turned out to rub her up the wrong way right from the start. Bella and Kate were always urging her to find someone new to help her get over Ben, and she knew that she ought to make more of an effort, but a man like Gib—always supposing he was available— was the last thing she needed. She wanted someone kind and reliable, someone she could trust, not someone who made her feel twitchy and inadequate just by sitting there, no matter *how* attractive he was.

'How do you know Josh?' she asked, when he made no effort to break the silence. 'You don't seem at all like him.'

'Don't I?' Gib looked amused. 'That depends how you think of Josh, I guess.'

'Josh is wonderful,' said Phoebe firmly. 'He's mainly Bella's friend, of course, but Kate and I love him. He seems so quiet, but he's one of the nicest people I know. He never shows off or boasts about how good he is at what he does. He's just steady and reliable and *safe*. Anything could happen, and you could always rely on Josh to know what to do.'

It was funny, she thought irrelevantly. Josh was just the kind of man she needed, but it had never crossed her mind to think of him as anything other than Bella's friend.

'Yes, he's very competent,' agreed Gib, reflecting wryly that he clearly hadn't made much of an impression so far. He wondered how Phoebe had decided that he was *not* quiet, or nice, or reliable like good old Josh. All he had done was admire her kitchen and accept a cup of tea.

'I met Josh in Ecuador,' he went on, thinking that this was not the time to challenge her for being unreasonable. 'He was leading an expedition up Mount Chimburazo, and I went along.'

She stared at him in surprise. 'You're a mountaineer?'

Gib smiled and shook his head, his blue, blue eyes looking directly into Phoebe's. 'No, I just like a challenge,' he said.

Trapped by the intense blue gaze, Phoebe felt a wave of heat wash through her, and she swallowed, jerking her eyes away with an effort.

There was something disconcerting about him, she thought with an edge of desperation. His presence seemed to fill the room, sucking in all the air until it was hard for her to breathe. His eyes were too bright, his teeth too white, and he was too vibrant, too unsettling, too everything.

Phoebe felt unbalanced, a bit dizzy, and, desperate for something to break the suddenly jarring atmosphere, she pushed her papers out of the way.

'Sorry about all this mess. I was just trying to do some work before the others got home.'

Gib twisted his head on one side to get a glimpse of the papers. 'What is that you do?'

'I'm a production assistant for a company that makes programmes for television,' said Phoebe, unable to keep the pride from her voice.

Of course, being little more than a dogsbody at her age wasn't that much to be proud about, but Phoebe had wanted to get into television production for as long as she could remember, and she was determined to make a success of it. Dogsbody was just the first step on the ladder, she reminded herself frequently. It was unfortunate that had ended up with a prima donna of the first order as her immediate boss, but Purple Parrot Productions was her big break, and it was worth putting up with Celia for that.

'We make documentaries mostly,' she told Gib.

'What are you working on at the moment?' he asked politely.

You never show any interest in my job, Mallory had complained. *You have no idea how to talk to a woman as a person in her own right. You only ever think about one thing.*

Which was absolute rubbish, of course, thought Gib. He was perfectly capable of talking to a woman seriously. Look at him now, asking Phoebe about her job and listening to her answer and not even thinking about the curve of her mouth or the silky sheen of her hair as she pushed it impatiently behind her ear.

Suddenly realising that he had lost track of what she was saying, Gib tuned in again to hear something about banking.

'You're making a programme about a *bank*?'

'I thought it was a pretty dull idea too,' said Phoebe, unsurprised by his reaction, 'but actually, it's more interesting than you'd expect. This isn't an ordinary bank. It was set up by some guy who made a fortune on the currency markets then took everyone by surprise by setting up an ethical bank.'

Gib put down his mug. 'What?'

'I know, it sounds like a contradiction in terms, doesn't it?' Phoebe had relaxed a bit in talking about her job. 'I think it just means that it only invests in community-based projects in developing countries. I've done some research on the internet, and it sounds really good. It should make an interesting programme.'

'Is that right?' said Gib in an odd voice.

'The only trouble is that my boss is insisting that the focus of the programme should be on the guy who set it all up.'

'Really? Who's that?'

'J.G. Grieve,' she told him. 'Everyone refers to him as JGG, and he's famous for not giving interviews to the media.' Picking up a printout from a website, she studied it ruefully. 'I've tried all these contact numbers, but I always get the same message: the bank is happy to support any publicity about the projects, but not about JGG himself.'

'So what else do you know about this guy?'

Preoccupied with her own problems, she failed to notice the oddly grim look around Gib's mouth. 'Not much,' she said. 'Just that he's very rich.'

'He's not that interesting then, is he?'

'That's what I think,' she agreed, 'but Celia—my boss—is insistent that I've got to arrange an interview somehow. Working on this programme is my big break, so I've got to track him down somehow. I'm just not quite sure how I'm going to go about it,' she confessed.

Gib looked at her across the table and suddenly his expression relaxed and his mouth quirked. 'Well, I've been in the States for a while,' he said. 'I know some people. Maybe

I could ask around and see if anyone knows anything else about him?'

Phoebe looked back doubtfully. She couldn't imagine that someone like Gib would have the kind of contacts she needed, but she supposed it was kind of him to offer.

'Well, thanks,' she said awkwardly, 'but I'm sure I'll get through to someone in the bank eventually.'

Gib grinned at her as he picked up his mug once more. 'Suit yourself,' he said.

There was a silence. Phoebe sipped her tea and tried not to feel rattled by the way he was sitting at her table, looking as if he had always sat there. His presence filled the kitchen, which seemed to have shrunk around them alarmingly.

'I gather from Josh that you're my landlady,' said Gib after a while. 'Thanks for letting me stay.'

When he smiled his eyes looked bluer than ever. Phoebe was more than ever convinced that they couldn't possibly be real. She looked away from them with an effort.

'That's all right,' she muttered.

'Are there any rules I should know about?'

Phoebe considered the question. 'Not really,' she said at last, 'but don't, whatever you do, tell Kate about any stray animal you've noticed unless you want to find it sleeping on your bed.'

'Is that it?'

'It's not a good idea to talk to me before I've had a cup of coffee in the morning, but that's advice rather than a rule,' she admitted. 'Kate and Bella don't take any notice of it.'

'Well, that seems easy enough,' said Gib. 'I ought to be able to manage that.'

He produced another of those unnervingly attractive smiles that seemed to linger in the air long after he had stopped, and Phoebe found herself getting to her feet abruptly. 'Shall I show you to your room?'

'It's not very big, I'm afraid,' she told him, opening a door off the upstairs landing.

'Not very big' was something of an understatement, reflected Gib, squeezing into the room behind Phoebe. It was not very big in the way the Sahara was not very wet, or the South Pole was not very hot.

An average cupboard might have been a better description, or possibly a large box. It had a four-foot bed, a built-in wardrobe, and a couple of shelves fixed to the wall. With the two of them standing on the only available floor space, there was absolutely no room for anything else.

'Out of interest, how long did your last room-mate live here?' asked Gib dryly.

'About a year. She was the last to move in, so she got the smallest room.'

Gib was glad to hear it. He would hate to think that anyone was sleeping in anything smaller!

'Caro didn't care,' said Phoebe a little defensively She could tell from his expression that he was less than overwhelmed with the room. 'She spent most of the time at her boyfriend's flat. They've just got married, which is why we're looking for someone to take her place.

'Obviously the rent is lower because you wouldn't have so much space,' she went on stiffly, 'but of course you don't have to take the room if it's too small.'

'No, no, it's fine,' Gib reassured her, perceiving that he had got off on the wrong foot. 'I haven't got much stuff. I travel light.'

Phoebe could believe it. He didn't look like the kind of man who bothered with baggage in any shape or form.

Part of her envied people like Gib who drifted carelessly through life avoiding commitment and responsibility and leaving others to clear up the broken hearts and disappointment they inevitably left in their wake, but another part was intimidated and more than a little irritated by them too.

'Yes, well, it's not as if you're staying for ever, is it?' she said briskly, wishing that Gib would move. The room was small enough at the best of times without him standing there vibrating with energy.

Short of climbing on the bed, which risked looking suggestive, let alone ridiculous, there was no way she could get past him without pressing intimately against him. The thought made Phoebe tense and shiver at the same time.

It was a sinful waste from one point of view, because it was a very long time since she had been this close to an attractive man, but there was something about the way he seemed constantly on the verge of exploding into action that made Phoebe nervous and edgy. Touching him, however inadvertently, seemed an action that would be downright rash.

She was just going to have wait until he moved.

Concentrating on breathing shallowly, she stood as close to the window as she could while Gib looked round. Given the size of the room, that didn't take long, but it felt like hours before he went back out onto the landing.

'Can I see the rest of the house?' he asked, and Phoebe was so relieved to be able to breathe properly again that she gave him a guided tour.

'It's a nice house,' said Gib as they went back downstairs. 'How long have you lived here?'

'A couple of years. I bought it with my fiancé, as he was then.' Phoebe was quite proud of the coolness in her voice. 'We lived here together for a year, and then Ben decided to move back to Bristol with someone he'd met, so I took over the mortgage.'

Gib didn't need to know about the anguish and the heartache and the long, long months of misery she had endured since Ben had left.

'I couldn't afford to live here on my own, so I had to take in lodgers, and it was just lucky that Kate was looking for somewhere at the same time. We were students together, and she knew Bella from school. Caro was a friend of Bella's, so it all worked out perfectly until Caro decided to get married. We're not sure where we're going to find any-one who fits in as well as she did,' she confessed as they went back into the kitchen.

'Can't you advertise?'

'We could, and that's probably what I'll end up doing, but it's hard to know what to put when you're really looking for someone who'll be a friend and not just a tenant.'

Mindful of his bet with Josh, Gib pricked up his ears at the key word. 'How do you know if someone is a friend?' he asked casually.

'That's just it, you don't,' said Phoebe. 'You can't tell who's going to be a good friend and who isn't. It's just something that clicks between you.'

Absently, she began piling her papers together to clear the table a bit, while she thought about Gib's question. 'I suppose a friend is someone who's easy to talk to, who laughs at the same things. Someone who's just going to fit in and be comfortable sitting around and talking all evening without wanting to organise us or worrying about how long it is since anyone got the hoover out.'

It was a bit vague, but Gib reckoned he could do all of that.

'Perhaps you should put that in your advert,' he suggested.

'I don't know that it would be much help. You could get someone who said they were able to do all those things, but you still might not get on. It's a funny thing, friendship,'

Phoebe mused. 'I don't think you can ever pin down the magic ingredient which makes you really like some people and not others.'

So much for picking up pointers from Phoebe! Gib sighed to himself. She was clearly *not* including him in her category of those with that special magic ingredient that would make him a friend!

Not yet, anyway.

Phoebe might be more of a challenge than he had anticipated, but challenges were there to be met. Gib wasn't giving up yet. He had a bet to win!

'How are you getting on with Gib?'

Josh and Phoebe were sitting on the sofa, while at the other end of the kitchen Bella and Kate busied themselves with the welcoming supper they had planned for Gib. Bella had told him that they were treating his welcome like the Queen's birthdays, so that he not only had the real one when he arrived, but the official dinner to mark the occasion a day later.

No effort was being spared. The table had been ruthlessly cleared of its clutter and ransacking the cupboards had revealed no less than four plates, in varying states of repair but with recognisably the same pattern.

'One of us can have the plate with the bunnies running round the edge,' said Bella breezily. 'We'll need to use one of the folding chairs from the garden, too.'

Now she and Kate were fussing over some elaborate starter, while Gib opened some wine and Phoebe and Josh, assigned to washing-up duty, had retired to a safe distance.

Phoebe looked over at Gib who was manipulating the corkscrew with practised ease. His head was bent and the lights gleaming on his hair made it look fairer than usual.

'Kate and Bella are completely smitten,' she told Josh.

'But not you?'

Phoebe looked away from Gib. 'I certainly wouldn't describe myself as smitten with him,' she said.

'Why, what's he done?'

That was the thing. Gib hadn't done anything. She couldn't even hold the taxi fare incident against him. He had repaid her in full without prompting that morning.

How could she explain to Josh how *unsettling* Gib was? He had only been in the house a day, but he was already firm friends with Bella and Kate, and lounged around the kitchen as if he had lived there for ever. Phoebe ought to have been relieved that he was fitting in so well, but instead she found herself edging nervously around him, as if afraid he was about to explode into action at any second.

'He's not very restful, is he?' she said to Josh, and he laughed.

'You just have to get used to him.'

Phoebe couldn't imagine ever getting used to Gib. Every time he came into the room she would catch her breath as if startled by the blueness of his eyes and the lazy good humour of his smile. Nobody had the right to be that attractive and that relaxed the whole time!

She wished she could be like Kate and Bella, and treat him like just another friend, but somehow she couldn't. You weren't aware of friends the way she was always aware of Gib.

It made Phoebe uneasy. There was nothing wrong with physical attraction, but it felt all wrong at the moment. She wasn't ready for another relationship, whatever her friends said. Ben had meant too much to her for her to get over him that easily. She might never get over him and, if she did, it certainly wasn't going to be with someone like Gib. He wasn't her type at all.

So why couldn't she get used to him as Josh suggested?

'I'll try,' she said.

Across the kitchen, Gib eased the cork out of the bottle with a satisfying pop and watched Phoebe talking to Josh. For the first time, he wondered if there might be something in this friendship thing. He had found himself envying Josh's uncomplicated friendship with the three girls, who were all patently delighted to see him. Even Phoebe's face had lit up, and she had given him an unselfconscious hug.

Gib sensed that she wasn't someone who hugged indiscriminately. It would be a real sign of acceptance if Phoebe hugged you, he thought. He could imagine with unnerving clarity what it would be like to feel her slender body in his arms, her silky hair against his cheek. He bet she smelt wonderful. He had noticed a faint scent lingering in the air after she had passed once or twice.

All right, every time.

Hugging Phoebe would be his goal, Gib decided. Just in a friendly way, of course, he added hastily to himself. It would be just like hugging Kate and Bella, both of whom had thrown their arms around him when they first met him.

They were both such warm, friendly open girls that it was impossible not to be friends with them. Gib already knew about Kate's obsession with someone referred to by Bella and Phoebe as Slimy Seb, and he had heard so much about Bella from Josh that she felt completely familiar.

But Phoebe…Phoebe was different. She was much more guarded and inclined to be prickly. Gib knew that he would have to work hard to earn her friendship and the prospect of a hug, but if he did, he thought it would be worth it.

Bella's Thai crab cakes to start were a huge success. Kate had roasted a chicken and Phoebe had been persuaded to make her trade mark strawberry torte in honour of the occasion. By the end of the meal, they were all replete and relaxed, and Gib felt as if he had been living there for ever.

'I'll make some coffee.' Phoebe pushed back her chair as Gib polished off the last of the torte. Unsettling he might be, but you had to admit that there was something very appealing about a man with a good appetite.

'How was Celia today?' asked Bella, sitting back with the air of one anticipating a good story.

Phoebe filled the kettle under the tap. 'Oh, the usual nightmare,' she sighed.

'Phoebe has the boss from hell,' Bella leant over to fill Gib in. 'Kate and I love hearing about her. It's sort of therapeutic. When you realise what Phoebe's going through with her immediate boss, it makes you realise that your own isn't that bad.'

'What's she done now?' Kate asked across Bella.

'She's completely obsessed with the man who runs this ethical bank we want to make a programme about. Now she's threatening to dump me from production work altogether if I can't fix up an interview with him!'

'She can't do that, can she?'

'It's such a small company, and so many people are desperate to work in television that she can pretty much do whatever she wants,' said Phoebe despairingly. 'Personally, I don't see why we can't just concentrate on the community projects which are the whole point of the bank, but Celia keeps banging on about the personal angle, and how this guy is the real story.

'I'm afraid she wants to do one of those horrible, cynical hatchet jobs,' she went on, opening and closing cupboard doors in search of the cafetière. 'Her theory is that nobody could make that kind of money and be truly altruistic, so if this J.G. Grieve is setting up a bank, it's because he's getting something out of it for himself. So I not only have to arrange an interview with him, I also have to dig up any dirt I can find on him so that Celia can challenge him with it and make herself look like a fearless investigative reporter.'

'Maybe there's no dirt to dig up,' said Gib lazily.

'It's beginning to look that way,' Phoebe agreed. 'All I've found out about him so far is that he goes climbing occasionally. It's hardly the stuff of which award-winning documentaries are made, is it?'

She poked through the debris on the counter. 'Where's the coffee gone?'

'In the fridge,' said Bella before reverting to the problem in hand. 'Maybe climbing is just the first clue you need to track him down,' she suggested. 'Mountaineering's quite a small world, isn't it, Josh? Someone might have come across him. These rich guys always need someone to nanny them when they do dangerous sports like that,' she added authoritatively, as if she had years of experience of dealing with the rich and famous.

'That's a good point.' Phoebe straightened from the fridge and turned back to the table. 'You're always running up and down mountains, Josh. Have you ever come across a J.G. Grieve?'

'I can't say the name means anything to me.' Josh looked across the table at Gib. 'What about you, Gib? You've done some climbing. Do you know anything about him.'

Tipping back in his chair, Gib pulled down the corners of his mouth. 'Bankers aren't the kind of guys I want to spend much time with,' he said. 'They're usually pretty boring.'

'Well, this guy can't be that boring, or why would he refuse all interviews?' Phoebe pointed out. 'Most people in his position would do anything for publicity. The fact that he won't even consider it does make it seem as if he's got something to hide. Maybe Celia's right about that.'

'There might be lots of reasons why he doesn't want to

talk to journalists,' objected Gib, still balanced precariously on his chair.

'Yes, maybe he had a terrible accident that left him scarred for life,' Kate put in. 'His wife died in the same accident, and their only child, and probably their dog as well.'

'Oh, no, not the dog as well!' said Gib, much struck by the story unfolding.

Kate nodded firmly. 'Yes, a little terrier. Called Ruffy,' she added as an afterthought. 'And you see that's why he's never been able to forgive himself. He's shut himself away from the world ever since then, unable to face anyone.'

There was a moment's silence, interrupted by Phoebe bringing the coffee back to the table.

'Kate has a very rich fantasy life,' she explained kindly to Gib. 'You'll get used to it.'

'Well, she convinced me,' he said. 'I think you should leave the poor guy alone and stop hassling him for an interview!'

'I wish I could,' sighed Phoebe. 'I'm sure that in reality he's really dull and avoiding interviews is just a way to try and make himself interesting. I think I'll tell Celia that I'm following leads, and hope that eventually she'll forget him.'

She held up the cafetière. 'Who's for coffee?'

'Any messages?' Kate asked hopefully, dropping her bag onto the table. It was over a week since their welcoming dinner for Gib, and she had come home to find Phoebe and Bella draped over the armchairs and nursing a glass of wine each as they grumbled about their respective bosses.

'No,' said Phoebe. 'And before you ask, yes, the phone *is* working! No post has been discovered under the doormat, there have been no emails or telegrams or bunches of flowers that accidentally got delivered to the wrong address six weeks ago. You've got to face it, Kate,' she said more gently. 'Seb's not going to ring.'

'But why is he being like this?' wailed Kate.

'Because he's vile,' said Bella firmly. 'Phoebe's right. Seb is never going to love anyone but himself. It suited him to string you along for a while, but he's obviously found someone new to exploit.'

Kate slumped into the sofa with a sigh. 'You don't think he was knocked over by a bus and lost his memory?'

'No.'

'Or had to go to his grandmother's funeral on a deserted island where all the phone lines are down and they're cut off because of storms?'

'What, for six weeks?'

'Well, maybe he's part of some top secret government programme where he's not allowed to contact anyone and—'

'No, Kate.'

She sighed again. 'I know, I know, it's probably not that. You're right, he's not going to call.'

Her eye fell on the cordless phone that was lying half buried under a pile of papers at the end of the sofa, and Phoebe and Bella both jerked upright as she reached for it.

'Kate, you are *not* going to ring him!'

'I'm just checking to see if anyone else called,' she said with dignity, pressing 1471. She listened to the number on the recorded message and her mouth drooped. 'No, it wasn't Seb. Some Bristol number I think.'

Phoebe dropped her head back with a groan. 'That'll be my mother. She wants to talk to me about Ben's wedding.'

'You're not really going to go to that, are you?' asked Bella curiously.

'I've got to,' she said. 'Ben's family and mine are so close, it would be like his sister not being at his wedding.'

'Still, they can't expect you to celebrate your fiancé marrying somebody else,' said Kate.

'They don't know it wasn't a mutual decision to break up,' Phoebe confessed. 'They were all so happy when Ben and I got engaged, I just couldn't bear to tell them. I love Penelope and Derek. Ben's parents are closer than any of my own aunts and uncles. They would have been devastated if I hadn't pretended that Ben and I had both agreed that it wasn't going to work.'

'They must have had a clue when he told them he was going to marry Lisa, surely?'

'He didn't tell them immediately. They might have suspected something, but I think they'd prefer to believe that I'm quite happy with the situation, so if I don't turn up they'll realise immediately that's not exactly the case.'

Phoebe ran her fingers through her hair in a hopeless gesture. 'Then *they'd* be upset, and it would spoil the wedding for them, and I can't do that to them. As it is, Penelope and Mum are desperately worried in case I'm embarrassed, or Ben is embarrassed, or Lisa is embarrassed...'

She sighed. 'I think they're secretly afraid that I might make some kind of scene when it comes down to it. I'm dreading going to the wedding on my own. It's bad enough at the best of times. You know what people are like about single women in their thirties, and it's going to be worse at this wedding since there'll be so many old friends there who all knew me when Ben and I were together.

'I know I'm going to end up looking like Glenn Close in *Fatal Attraction*. Either people are going to be edging warily around me and making sure any stray bunnies are safe, or they'll be desperately sorry for me. I'll spend my whole time being told cheerily that it will be my turn next,' she finished gloomily.

'It's dire, isn't it?' said Kate with heartfelt sympathy. 'It's either that or being asked if it isn't time you were thinking of getting married—like you've got some kind of choice in the matter!'

Bella had been pondering the problem. 'What you need,' she said, 'is a man.'

'Tell us something new!'

'No, I'm serious. You should take a fabulous lover to show off at the wedding.'

'Oh, yes, and fabulous lovers are *so* easy to find!' said Kate sarcastically. 'Didn't you hear the announcement? It's now official: there are now no single, straight men over thirty at all in London, let alone any with a modicum of intelligence and financial stability. And as for trying to find one not suffering from a morbid fear of commitment…forget it!'

'Maybe not,' said Bella, 'but there's nothing to stop Phoebe inventing one.'

CHAPTER THREE

FOR a moment there was utter silence, and then Kate looked at Bella with new respect. 'That's a brilliant idea, Bel!' she said.

Phoebe was less impressed. 'I don't see that an imaginary lover is going to do me much good, however fabulous he is!'

'The whole point is that he doesn't *seem* to be imaginary,' said Bella. 'All you need is to hire someone to pretend to be a lover as fabulous as you want!'

'You don't mean hire a male escort?' Phoebe stared at her, appalled. 'I couldn't do that!'

'I'm not suggesting that you pick up some gigolo,' said Bella reasonably. 'I bet you're not the first woman to need an escort in this kind of situation. There must be some reputable agencies that supply presentable types who are used to going along to weddings and official dinners. You'd have to pay for it, of course, but there wouldn't have to be any funny business.'

'Yes, and since you're paying him, you could get him to say whatever you wanted,' Kate added eagerly, picking up the idea and running with it with typical enthusiasm.

'He's bound to be good-looking if he works for an escort agency, so you could pretend he's incredibly rich and successful, too. You can tell everyone that he utterly adores you, and asks you to marry him every day, but you're not sure whether he's *exactly* what you want, so you're keeping him dangling.'

'Why would I want to do that?'

'So everyone will envy you, of course. The other women at the wedding, anyway,' Kate qualified. 'And the best thing is that if anyone meets you in the future and asks what's happened to him, you can say that you just got bored with his insatiable sexual demands!'

Phoebe couldn't help laughing. 'That doesn't sound very likely!'

'OK, he can't satisfy *your* insatiable appetite!'

'Oh, yes, I can see myself telling Mum that when she asks why I don't bring my nice young man down for the weekend!'

'Kate's just complicating things,' said Bella, bringing them back to order. 'All you need is someone attractive who will brush up nicely in a suit and look suitably adoring so that instead of everyone pitying you or making their husbands and boyfriends cover their eyes whenever you go near them, they'll all be madly jealous!'

Phoebe let herself imagine what it would be like to turn up at Ben's wedding with someone apparently rich and good-looking on her arm. She had to admit that as an idea, it had its advantages. Her mother and Penelope would relax and enjoy the wedding for a start, and there was no doubt that it would be easier to meet Ben and Lisa if she wasn't quite so obviously left on the shelf.

'I'm not sure I would have the nerve to carry it off,' she said doubtfully.

Bella was having none of that. 'Of course you would,' she said briskly. 'Now, the first thing is for you to start dropping a few hints to your mother that you've met someone special, and then we've just got to find you a man and get him primed up with your story.'

'I don't know...' said Phoebe feebly, half dazzled and half terrified by the way Bella and Kate were sweeping her along on the tide of their enthusiasm.

They were always doing this, pushing her into doing things and then holding up their hands in innocence when the said things turned out to be a terrible mistake.

The colour of the bathroom paint—a lurid pink they had assured her would look fantastic—was a case in point.

Ignoring her feeble attempts to come up with some sensible objections—Phoebe was sure there had to be thousands, if she could only think of them—Kate and Bella were discussing how best to track down a reputable escort agency.

'I suppose we could try the obvious and look in the Yellow Pages,' said Bella eventually. 'Where are they, anyway?'

She started hunting through the pile of clutter on the table. 'I'm sure I saw them here the other day. God, we must tidy up soon, I can't find anything—oh, that's where my glove is!' She fished it out triumphantly and tossed it onto the sofa, where it promptly slipped down out of sight once more.

'Aha!' she cried, spotting the directory, dragging it free of a welter of paper and beginning to flick through it without much system. 'What do I look under? A for agency or E for escorts?'

'Hold on,' said Kate slowly. 'I've got a better idea.'

Bella looked sceptical. 'Not another of your elaborate fantasies?'

'No, no, this is so simple and so obvious I don't know why neither of you thought of it,' she insisted. 'Why go through an agency when we've got the perfect candidate living right here in the house?'

'Who?'

'Gib, of course!'

Kate sat back and beamed, delighted with her own brilliance.

'Gib?'

The other two stared at Phoebe's outraged tone. 'I never knew you could do such a good Lady Bracknell impression!' said Bella, diverted.

Phoebe shot her a look. 'I'm not asking Gib!'

'Why not? You've got to admit, he's incredibly attractive.'

'He's not that special,' she protested, unwilling to admit anything of the kind.

'Oh, come on, Phoebe!' Kate rolled her eyes in disbelief. 'He's gorgeous, and you know it!'

Phoebe's mouth set in a stubborn line. 'He's too pleased with himself,' she said, 'and I'm sure he must wear contact lenses. Nobody has eyes that blue!'

'Don't be silly, of course they're real,' said Kate. 'You're not doing much of a job of not finding him attractive if the only thing you can think of to say is that his eyes are too blue!'

'I can see that he's quite good-looking,' Phoebe allowed grudgingly. 'I just think he would be more attractive if he didn't know it.'

Kate shook her head. 'I don't understand why you don't like him,' she said, puzzled. 'I think he's great. He's good fun, he's easy to talk to, he does his bit around the house, and he doesn't roll his eyes at the mess or insist on correcting you if you say it's about five hundred miles to somewhere when in fact he knows it's four hundred and ninety-seven.'

'Well, don't you think that's a bit fishy?' countered Phoebe. 'He's just a little *too* perfect, if you ask me. Why hasn't he got a girlfriend if he's that wonderful?'

'Maybe he's gay,' said Bella dubiously.

'He's definitely not that.' Phoebe's voice held a tart edge as she thought of the way Gib flirted with everyone from the plump checkout woman at the supermarket, to the elderly lady who lived next door and the newsagent's shy wife. Flirtation obviously came as naturally as breathing to him, an automatic response to any female that crossed his path.

Except her, of course. He never flirted with her.

'I'd prefer him if he was,' she said.

'I don't think he's gay either,' said Kate. 'Maybe he's got a broken heart like the rest of us,' she added with a sigh.

'He's doing a good job of concealing it, then,' said Phoebe, unconvinced. 'He's always smiling, even when he's not.'

They blinked at her curiously. 'What?'

'You know.' Too late, she heard how obscure she sounded.

'No.'

'Yes, you do,' she insisted, a little embarrassed now. 'Even when he's got a perfectly straight face, you get the feeling he's laughing at you.'

'Phoebe, it's called having a sense of humour,' said Bella as if explaining to a child. 'And how many men do we know who need one of those? If only they were all like Gib, life would be a lot easier!'

Phoebe was beginning to get frustrated. Her friends just didn't seem to be able to understand how jittery Gib made her feel.

She picked morosely at the arm of her chair, trying to find the words to explain. 'He's just so *vague* about everything,' was the best she could come up with. 'We don't really know anything about him, do we? I mean, what does he *do* all day? He talks about these unspecified projects of his, but as far as I can see he spends his entire time lounging around here.'

'Well, he's got a laptop and a mobile phone,' Kate

pointed out in an infuriatingly reasonable voice. 'He can probably work just as effectively from here as going in to some office.'

'He doesn't look like he's working to me. I've never met anyone as lazy!'

'He's relaxed. That's a good sign.'

'No one's got the right to be that relaxed,' grumbled Phoebe, determined not to be convinced.

'Look, aren't we getting from the point?' Bella interrupted, chinking a teaspoon against her glass for their attention. 'Say what you like, Phoebe, but the fact is that Kate's right. Gib would be ideal. He looks good, he's got the confidence to carry the whole thing off, and the best thing is that he's actually living here, so if your mother or anyone rings and he answers phone, it would be dead convincing!'

'Maybe, but—'

'And I'm sure he would be willing to help you,' Kate chipped in before Phoebe had a chance to think up any more objections. 'You could always offer to pay him if that made you feel better. I get the impression he could do with some extra money and it would be a way of helping him out without hurting his pride.'

'Oh, yes, let's worry about Gib's pride!' said Phoebe sarcastically. 'What about *mine*?'

'Just think of it as a business arrangement,' said Bella. 'It's all it would be, after all. You were prepared to go to an escort agency, and who knows what kind of psychopath you could end up with there? At least Gib would be a better option than that!'

Phoebe opened her mouth to point out that she hadn't in fact got anywhere near agreeing to the idea of hiring an escort, but the sound of the front door banging made her stop.

Bella smiled triumphantly as if she had just won the argument. 'Here's Gib now,' she said unnecessarily. 'You can at least ask him, Phoebe.'

A few moments later, Gib himself breezed into the kitchen. As usual, he brought with him a surge of energy that swirled around the room as if a fresh wind had blown in with him, and as usual Phoebe found herself braced against the impact of his smile.

'Hey, girls,' he said and lifted a carrier bag in their direction. 'I bought more tonic.'

'You see!' whispered Kate. 'How can you say he's not perfect?'

Phoebe pretended not to hear. Draining her glass, she began to get to her feet. She was *not* going to let Kate and Bella push her into this stupid idea. There was nothing wrong with going to Ben's wedding on her own!

'Gib, we were just talking about you,' said Bella.

'Oh?' Gib turned from the fridge where he was stacking the bottles of tonic.

'Phoebe's got something to ask you.'

Jerking upright, Phoebe glared at her friend. '*Bel*-la,' she said warningly.

'Look Phoebe, you've been going on and on about how much you're dreading this wedding,' Bella said in a firm voice. 'You were worried about your pride. Well, here's a way to get through it with your pride intact. What's the harm in at least asking Gib?'

Gib looked from one to the other. 'Ask me what?'

'Come on, Kate, we'll let Phoebe ask him herself,' said Bella, getting up. 'We'll leave you two alone, and then she can tell you it's all our fault,' she added kindly to Gib, who raised an amused eyebrow and turned to Phoebe with an enquiring look.

She put up her chin. 'I don't want to ask you anything,' she said bravely, but Kate and Bella had already whisked out of the door, and she couldn't follow them because Gib was standing in front of it, his blue eyes alight with that disturbing laughter that never failed to send the air leaking out of her lungs.

'Yes,' he said.

Phoebe looked blankly at him. 'Yes, what?'

'Yes, I'll do whatever it is you want me to do.'

'But you don't know what it is yet!'

'Is it illegal?'

'Of course not!'

'Immoral?'

'No!'

Gib shrugged. 'Then why would I refuse?'

To her chagrin, Phoebe realised she had been manoeuvred into beginning to talk about Kate and Bella's idea with Gib, *exactly* the thing she hadn't wanted to happen! But she could hardly walk out in mid-conversation.

'Because it's embarrassing,' she muttered.

'For you or for me?'

'For both of us.'

'This is beginning to sound like fun!'

Gib strolled over towards her, and Phoebe found herself backing down into her chair once more. 'Come on,' he said encouragingly, sitting on the arm of the sofa. 'You've got this far, so you might as well tell me the worst!'

He wasn't anywhere near her, but Phoebe was desperately aware of him. She wished he'd go back to the fridge. If only he wasn't so...so *overwhelming*.

'It was just a silly idea,' she mumbled.

'All the best ideas are silly to start with,' said Gib. 'If they were sensible, somebody else would have thought of them before.'

'Well, this one really is silly,' she told him almost belligerently.

He smiled. 'Why don't you let me be the judge of that?'

Phoebe tore her eyes away from the warm blue eyes and scowled at the mess on the table.

'All right,' she said, giving in. 'I need a lover.'

There was a tiny silence. 'In that case, I'm glad I said yes,' said Gib, and although she wasn't looking at him, she could hear him smiling and the colour deepened in her cheeks.

'Not a real one! Don't be stupid,' she snapped.

'Right,' he said, humouring her.

'The thing is…' Somehow Phoebe stumbled through the whole sorry saga of Ben's wedding and her attempts to keep everyone in the family happy. 'So we were wondering—it was Kate's idea, I'd never have thought of it—and it's entirely up to you, of course—you can say no, it won't be a problem at all….'

She floundered to a halt, lost in a morass of sentences, and looked a little helplessly at Gib, who was studying her with a disconcerting half-smile.

'Well, I've already said yes, so I'm sure it won't be a problem,' he agreed, 'but I'm still not entirely clear what it is you want me to do, other than *not* be a real lover.'

Wasn't it *obvious*? Phoebe was hating this. If she had to spell it out for him, she would, but she couldn't help resenting Gib for not being able to make immediate sense of her incoherent ramblings.

'OK.' She drew a breath. 'I wondered if you'd be interested in earning some extra cash, that's all.'

Gib's brows rose. 'You're offering me a *job*?' he said blankly.

'We had the impression that things weren't very easy for you at moment,' said Phoebe stiffly, borrowing Kate's comment. 'In the circumstances, I'd be prepared to pay you to come to wedding with me and pretend…well, pretend…'

'That I'm in love with you?' he finished for her, a smile lurking around his mouth, and she let out a breath that she hadn't been aware until then that she had been holding.

'Yes.'

His lips twitched. 'You want me to be a male escort?'

'Yes.'

There, it was out. Phoebe sat back, oddly relieved. Maybe Kate and Bella were right. He could only say no, and when it came down to it, all she had done was offer him a chance to earn some extra money. What was so embarrassing about that?

'Well, I've never been offered a job like that before!' Gib shook his head, but he was grinning.

'It would be just a job, of course,' said Phoebe hastily. 'There wouldn't be any...any of the reason why you might normally pay for a male escort.' She could feel the treacherous colour creeping back up into her cheeks. So much for not being embarrassed! 'I'd be paying you to be an actor, that's all.'

Gib didn't answer immediately. 'You know, Phoebe, you don't need to pay me,' he said carefully at last. 'We're friends, aren't we? If Josh was sitting here now, you wouldn't even think of offering him money to help you, would you?'

It was true, of course. Phoebe wished that she *had* been able to ask Josh. He was so nice and reliable, he would have been ideal, but unfortunately her parents had already met him and knew about his friendship with Bella. They would never believe that she had come between those two.

Gib wasn't like Josh. He wasn't calm and he wasn't *safe*. He didn't make her feel comfortable the way Josh did. Phoebe couldn't think of him as a friend like Josh when all her nerves jangled and twitched the moment he walked into the room. Friends were people you could relax and be yourself with, not people who made you feel as if the earth was unsteady beneath your feet.

'I'd feel more comfortable if we both thought of this as a financial transaction,' she said firmly. 'That way I'll be able to ask you to do things I wouldn't want to ask if you were just doing me a favour.'

'Like what?'

'Like...' Phoebe didn't really want to get into what she might have to ask him to do to convince her family they really were in love. 'Well, I can't think of anything right now,' she prevaricated, 'but there's sure to be something. Anyway, it's already asking a lot for you to give up a whole day to spend it at a wedding with a load of people you don't know.'

'I'll know you,' Gib pointed out, unperturbed by the prospect.

'You'll have to get to know me a lot better before you can face an interrogation by my mother!' she warned him.

Gib's mouth quirked in a smile. 'I'll look forward to it.'

There was an odd little silence.

That was the thing about Gib, Phoebe thought edgily. He would say something perfectly innocuous like that, and suddenly the whole atmosphere had changed without you realising how or why it had happened.

She cleared her throat and strove for a businesslike tone. 'Well, as I say, I'd prefer to keep it a business arrangement. I'll pay you for your time, and also for the hire of a suit and anything else you might need.'

Her face was scarlet by this stage. Gib hesitated. The last thing he wanted was to take money from Phoebe, but he could see what it had cost her to ask him to help her. Paying him was a way of saving her pride, and if he argued with her, it would only prolong her embarrassment. It wasn't as if he had to do anything with the money, and he could always find a way to give it back to her later.

Meanwhile, here was the perfect opportunity to prove to all those Doubting Thomases like Mallory and Josh that he was just as good a friend as the next person. Phoebe needed him, and he wouldn't let her down. He would be doing this for her.

The fact that helping her would mean spending a day in close proximity was purely incidental. If he had to touch her, maybe even kiss her, as part of the pretence, well, that was hardly his fault, Gib reasoned virtuously. It was just a lucky side effect of being a friend, and Josh wouldn't be able to claim that he had broken the terms of their bet.

'OK, if that's what you want,' he said briskly, deciding that it would make things much easier for her if he played along with the idea that he needed the money. At least that way, she could think that she was doing him a favour too. 'You're the boss. How much were you thinking of paying me?'

'Well, I don't really know...' Phoebe was a bit taken aback by his abrupt volte-face. 'I suppose I could ring an agency and find out how much one of their escorts would cost,' she offered awkwardly, conscious of a quite unfair sense of disappointment that he had turned out to be interested in the money after all. He must need some extra cash very badly. 'I could pay you the same.'

'It's a deal,' said Gib and leant forward to offer his hand to seal the bargain.

Phoebe looked at it, stupidly reluctant to put hers into it, but she couldn't think of a good reason to refuse, and it would only look rude if she ignored it. So instead she put her hand out, bracing herself against the cool strength of his grasp and the tingling warmth of his palm pressed against hers.

'Right.' Gib released her just as she began to think that it didn't feel that bad after all. He was abruptly all business. 'Tell me again exactly what it is you want me to do.'

'I'm going to tell my mother that I've met someone special,' said Phoebe, marvelling at how easily she had been swept along into the whole idea. Hadn't she decided only a few minutes ago that she wanted nothing to do with it? Oh, well, she might as well go with the flow. Resisting the combined will of Bella, Kate and Gib would be just too exhausting.

'If I know Mum, she'll be straight on the phone to Penelope—that's Ben's mother—and you can bet your bottom dollar that an invitation to the wedding will be dropping through the door for you five minutes later.'

She hesitated. 'The thing is, if my mother rings up in the meantime, and you answer the phone for some reason, you'll have to be prepared to be cross-examined by her. Would you mind that?'

'That's what you're paying me for,' said Gib cheerfully.

Phoebe knew that she ought to be reassured by his down-to-earth approach, but somehow the fact that he was treating it as a job, just as she had insisted he should, was a bit disconcerting.

'Yes…well…' she said, somewhat at a loss. 'Then, obviously, there's the wedding itself. That's when the real pretence comes in.'

'The pretending to be in love with you?'

'That, too, but I was thinking more of you pretending to have a proper job or something. After all, if I'm going to make up a lover, I might as well make up an incredibly successful one.'

'Ah,' said Gib, looking down at himself, his would-be regretful expression marred by the twitch of his lips. 'That might be more of a problem,' he sighed. 'I can see why it would be good for you to have a wealthy and successful lover, but do you think I'd be able to carry off an image like that?'

Phoebe surveyed him with a critical eye. He was lounging on the arm of the sofa, wearing jeans and a battered leather jacket over a plain white T-shirt that stretched across his broad chest. Laughter lines fanned his eyes and creased his cheeks, and the blue, blue eyes danced. He looked vibrant and physical and—OK, Kate—attractive, and absolutely nothing like a businessman.

Her mouth turned down at the corners. 'Maybe if you cut your hair,' she suggested doubtfully, 'and generally brush up a bit. A suit would make a difference, too. You'd better hire one before the wedding.'

'It's going to be a smart wedding, then?' asked Gib, not unduly put out by her critical appraisal.

'Yes,' said Phoebe without enthusiasm. 'The wedding party is taking over an entire castle. It's been turned into a hotel, where all the rooms have panelling and four-poster beds, you know the kind of thing.'

'Aren't they getting married in a church?'

'No, the ceremony is at the castle as well, so that everyone moves straight on to the reception in the gardens. And then close friends and family are staying on for dinner and dancing in the evening. This will be a more intimate affair, according to my mother, and they've booked all the rooms in the castle, so I've got to get through all of that and breakfast next morning, as if the wedding itself wasn't going to be bad enough,' she finished glumly.

Gib raised an eyebrow. 'So we'll be spending the night?'

'I'll have to, but we can think of some excuse for you. I'll tell them you have to get back that evening because you've got a meeting the next day.'

'On a Sunday?'

'Not everyone has your relaxed attitude to work,' Phoebe retorted. 'It's a well-known fact that all successful businessmen are workaholics! I don't think anyone would be surprised to hear that you had a weekend meeting.'

'Right, well, I'll bow to your superior knowledge on that one,' said Gib. 'What sort of businessman am I supposed to be, anyway, in case anyone asks?'

'We hadn't got that far,' she admitted. 'What would you like to be?'

'Perhaps I could say that I'm in…oh, I don't know…' He scratched his chin thoughtfully. 'What about banking?'

Phoebe looked doubtful. 'You don't think you should pretend to be something less…ambitious?' she said carefully.

'What do you mean?' Gib pretended to be affronted. 'You don't think I look like a banker?'

'Not really.'

'Hey, I can put on a suit and poker up with the best of them!' he reassured her, but Phoebe was unconvinced.

'I don't know that it's such a good idea,' she said. 'Ben works for one of those big international tax consultancy firms, and the reception will be choc-a-bloc with City types. You know what men are like about sniffing out each other's status. If you say you're in banking they're bound to ask who you work for, what kind of bonuses you earn and how many Ferraris you've got sitting in your garage, and what are you going to say then?'

'I'll say I've been working for some American bank,' said Gib easily. 'Relax, it'll be fine.'

Phoebe wasn't so sure, but she told herself that she could always tell her mother that he had come down with an acute case of food poisoning if necessary and go on her own as she'd planned.

'When is this wedding?' he asked, still in business-like mode.

'In three weeks.'

'That's fine then,' he said. 'I'll have plenty of time to prepare my role.'

He seemed so casual about the whole thing, as if women asked him to pretend to be in love with them every day of the week. Phoebe chewed her thumb nervously.

'Are you *sure* you don't mind doing this?' she asked, abruptly attacked by doubts.

'Why would I mind?' said Gib. 'It's a chance to earn some extra cash and drink champagne at someone else's expense. It'll be fun.'

It wasn't Phoebe's idea of fun. She felt tense at the mere thought of carrying off the deception. 'Frankly, at the moment sticking pins in my eyeballs seems like more fun,' she said.

'Then don't do it.'

Phoebe thought about turning up at the wedding on her own, and how awkward it would be for her family and for Ben's. 'No, I want to do it,' she said, making up her mind. 'It will make everyone happy if they see that I seem to have found someone else.'

'Everyone except you,' Gib pointed out.

She looked at the cat curled up on the sofa. 'I've got used to not being happy since Ben left,' she said bleakly.

There was a pause. 'You're still in love with him,' said Gib, sounding oddly flat.

Phoebe kept her eyes on the cat. 'Ben's part of my life,' she answered him after a moment. 'We were toddlers together. I planned to marry him when I was four, and I never wanted anyone else. I suppose I took it for granted that he would always be there for me, and now I can't get used to the fact that he isn't.'

In spite of herself, her voice wobbled treacherously, and Gib saw her lift her chin to an unconsciously gallant tilt. 'I

know Ben didn't want to hurt me but I've accepted the fact
that he loves Lisa, not me. Now I just want him to be happy,
and if that means pretending to be in love with someone
else at his wedding, that's what I'll do.'

Most of the women Gib had known would have given in
to bitterness or rage at their disappointed dreams, but not
Phoebe. He wanted to tell her how brave he thought she
was, but he was afraid that she would be mortified if she
thought that he had glimpsed her distress.

'If that's what you want,' he said, getting to his feet instead, 'I'm happy to do my bit to help. I won't let you
down.'

Caught unawares by the sincerity in his voice, Phoebe
glanced at him and saw that the blue eyes were warm with
sympathy, almost as if he could see the painful lump of
unshed tears in her throat. 'Thank you,' she said with difficulty.

'Hey, no problem.'

Murmuring something about a shower, he left her alone
with the cat.

Phoebe looked after him with a curious expression. 'What
do you think about that?' she asked the cat, who deigned to
open one yellow eye in case food was in the offing. 'Who
would have thought Gib would be that tactful?'

The cat yawned hugely, uninterested. Phoebe reran the
conversation with Gib in her mind. He had been surprisingly
understanding. He hadn't probed for details about her break
up with Ben or made fun of her predicament, and now her
resistance to asking him to help her was beginning to seem
a bit churlish.

She wasn't sure how he was going to carry off being a
banker, but otherwise Kate was right, he was the perfect
person to help her. He had been nice about it, too. Phoebe
watched the cat stretching and remembered how Gib had

smiled. *I'm glad I said yes*, he had said when she told him that she needed a lover. *I'll look forward to it.*

The memory sent an odd feeling snaking down her spine, and she got abruptly to her feet. Anticipating the chance of being fed, the cat jumped down and headed purposefully to its bowl, where it sat and fixed Phoebe with faintly menacing yellow eyes.

'Oh, all right,' she sighed, fully aware that any movement towards the fridge would mean her ankles passing well within biting range. It went against the grain to give in but she cravenly shook some biscuits into its bowl. It was obviously her night for giving in.

What would it be like, spending the whole day with Gib? Phoebe was uneasily conscious of a tremble of anticipation uncurling somewhere deep inside her at the prospect. Ridiculous, of course. OK, so he had been nicer than expected, and at lot less irritating than usual, but that was no reason to forget that the arrangement they had made was a strictly businesslike one.

'Don't worry, I'm not going to do anything silly,' Phoebe informed the cat as if it had objected. 'There's no question of me getting involved with Gib.'

And there wasn't, she reassured herself. Gib wasn't the sort of man sensible girls like her fell in love with. He might be fun for a while, but he would move on eventually, and it would hurt. When Phoebe thought about the pain of the past year since Ben had left, she knew that she wasn't prepared to risk that again. If she did ever let herself fall in love again, she would have to be very, very sure that it would be for ever, and Gib just wasn't a for ever kind of guy.

'No, I'm grateful to him for helping me out,' Phoebe told the cat firmly, 'but that's all.'

CHAPTER FOUR

IN SOME ways, that conversation with Gib left Phoebe feeling even more unsettled than ever. It had been easier when he was irritating, she thought, and when the days passed with no sign that he was doing anything about preparing for his role, she was almost relieved to find herself getting quite cross again.

It was all very well for Gib to lounge around the kitchen joking with Bella and Kate, but he seemed to have no idea of how easily he could be revealed as a fraud, Phoebe fretted, her gratitude eking away with each fresh onset of nerves. Of course she appreciated how understanding he had been, but when it came down to it, she *was* paying him, and the least he could do was make an effort to seem convincing at the wedding.

Kate and Bella pooh-poohed her worries, but then *they* weren't risking humiliation in front of their family and oldest friends, were they? If anyone at the wedding discovered that Gib was not in fact the banker he claimed to be, her cover would be blown too. She would be revealed as a sad, pathetic spinster who was reduced to paying a man to pretend to be in love with her.

Phoebe cringed at the prospect. She couldn't stop thinking about everything that could go wrong, and had lived through each potentially disastrous scenario so many times that she could picture every one down to the last detail.

There was the banker who quizzed Gib about exchange rate mechanisms and investment portfolios with increasing puzzlement until he exclaimed, 'Damn it, I don't think you're a banker at all!' just as a hush fell on the gathering. Phoebe shuddered at the thought of everyone turning to stare at Gib, who would be left blustering unconvincingly.

Or one of the other guests might know Gib. It was all very well for him to say that he had been in the States for the past few years, but people travelled and coincidences happened all the time. What was the betting one of his old surfing pals would be there, only too ready to throw back his head and hoot with laughter at the idea of Gib being a banker?

Sometimes Phoebe varied the theme, and imagined one of his ex-girlfriends turning up at the wedding with one of Ben's friends, and spotting an ideal opportunity to wreak her revenge on him. There would be champagne thrown in his face, tears and tantrums and accusations as Gib's past caught up with him…oh, yes, she could see it all.

But the scenario Phoebe dreaded most was the one where it gradually dawned on her parents that the man masquerading as their daughter's lover knew nothing about her and cared even less. If they guessed that she was deceiving them, they would be desperately hurt. Her mother would tell Penelope, who would tell Ben, who would obviously tell Lisa, and before she knew it, word would go round the reception like wildfire. Already Phoebe could picture the whispered asides, the pitying glances, the way the conversation would fall awkwardly silent as soon as she approached, and she cringed as if it was already happening.

After nights spent churning over one humiliating scenario after another, she had just decided to call the whole thing off when she let herself into the house one evening to find Gib chatting cosily to her mother on the phone in the kitchen.

'To tell you the truth, Mrs Lane,' he was saying in a confidential tone, 'I knew the moment I saw Phoebe. It was like a bolt from the blue. I just looked at her and knew that she was the woman I wanted to spend the rest of my life with!'

Phoebe's mouth dropped open before she recovered sufficiently to snatch the receiver from Gib's hand. 'Mum!' she said on a gasp. 'Sorry, I've just got in.'

'That's all right, dear. I've been having a nice little chat with Gib. I must say, he sounds absolutely charming!'

Her voice was clearly audible, and Gib sent Phoebe a smug grin. Pointedly, she turned her back on him.

'We can't wait to meet him,' her mother was burbling happily on. 'Penelope was thrilled when I told her, and she said she would send an invitation off straight away. Did Gib get it?'

An embossed white card had dropped through the door practically the day after Phoebe had rung her mother to drop Gib's name into the conversation for the first time. She must have been straight on the phone to Penelope. Phoebe could picture Ben's mother frantically gesturing for a pen so that she could write out the invitation there and then.

'Yes, we got it,' she said. 'I'm not sure Gib will be able to spend the night, though,' she went on quickly, anticipating her mother's next question. She might as well knock that idea on the head right now. Her nerves were going to be in shreds as it was, without the prospect of spending the night with Gib as well.

'Oh, what a pity!' Her mother was clearly disappointed. 'You know what receptions are like. We won't get a chance to relax and talk to him properly until the evening.'

Relaxing and talking properly was precisely what Phoebe didn't want. That would be the very time they were likely to let slip a comment that brought the whole pretence crashing down around them. No, much better to get Gib firmly out of the way.

'I know, but Gib's got to work the next day, I'm afraid,' she said, trying to force some regret into her voice.

Her mother clicked her tongue impatiently. She had no time for the tedious business of actually earning a living. 'I'm sure he can work another time,' she said, and then to Phoebe's acute embarrassment lowered her voice. 'You know it's not a problem about you two sharing a room, don't you? Penelope's absolutely fine about it. We know things are different for your generation.'

'It's not that, Mum,' said Phoebe, squirming and hoping Gib couldn't hear. He hadn't even had the decency to leave the kitchen to let her talk to her mother in peace, and she was very conscious of him lounging on the sofa behind her, hands behind his head and long legs crossed.

'It's just that he's got a meeting in…um…' Oh, God, where did bankers have meetings? '…in…er, in…yes, Switzerland,' she remembered triumphantly after a nasty moment where her mind went completely blank. 'It's first thing the next day, so he'll have to get back.'

'Oh, well, if he must, he must.' Her mother made no attempt to hide her disappointment, and Phoebe sighed inwardly, spotting a fresh attack of guilt coming on.

'But do try and see if he can change his meeting,' her mother went on, working up to the emotional blackmail. 'We're all so looking forward to getting to know him. It's not just your father and I. Lara's very keen to meet him, too.'

Phoebe closed her eyes briefly. Lara was her younger sister. She had a sweet, pretty face and could be disconcertingly perceptive at times. Phoebe would have to keep her well away from Gib. She would see through him in a second.

'I'll ask him,' she lied. 'I'm sure he'll see what he can do.'

'This is turning into a nightmare,' she sighed as she switched off the phone and threw it onto a chair. 'I wish I'd never mentioned you to my mother!'

'Why?' said Gib. 'It seems to be working perfectly. You wanted your mother to be happy, and she is.'

This was unanswerable. Phoebe made a show of looking through the post she had brought in from the hall. A credit card bill, two circulars and a letter from the gym asking plaintively why they hadn't seen her for a while.

'Why did you tell Mum all that stuff about love at first sight?' she demanded instead.

'I thought I was supposed to be a besotted lover,' said Gib.

'Not that besotted! Nobody's going to believe you if you carry on like that!'

'Why not?'

'Well, because it doesn't happen like that in real life, does it?' she said, a bit thrown by the directness of Gib's question.

'What doesn't?'

'All that bolt from the blue stuff. You have to know someone before you can fall in love with them.'

Gib looked at her, one corner of his long, mobile mouth curling upwards in a crooked smile. 'That might be true for you, but it isn't necessarily the same for everyone else.'

'Don't tell me you've ever fallen in love at first sight!' said Phoebe, tearing up the letter from the gym and dropping the credit card bill onto the table unopened.

'Why shouldn't I have done?'

It was a fair enough question. 'You don't seem the type,' was the best she could do for an answer.

'That's what I thought until it happened to me.'

'Oh.' She eyed him a little uncertainly, wishing, not for the first time, that she could tell whether he was joking or not. He could keep his mouth perfectly straight as now, but it always seemed on the verge of twitching upwards, and as for those eyes...Phoebe risked a glance only to find herself skewered by a blue gleam that was impossible to interpret but which for some reason sent the blood surging into her cheeks.

She jerked her gaze away. 'Are you sure was it was love and not lust?' she said, trying to be ironic but succeeding only in sounding tremulous.

'I think it was a bit of both,' said Gib.

He smiled then, a reminiscent smile that turned up the corners of his mouth and creased the edges of his eyes. No doubt thinking of some long-legged, sun-streaked blonde he had met lazing around on a Californian beach, thought Phoebe, inexplicably irritable.

Turning her back on that smile, she headed over to the fridge, her dignified demeanour rather spoilt by falling over the cat who had been waiting to ambush the next human who approached his bowl.

'The point is, I'm trying to convince my family here,' she said coldly, disentangling herself from the weaving cat with difficulty and opening the fridge door, relieved to see a bottle of wine that had been chilling overnight. She could do with a drink! 'We need to stick to a realistic scenario, or they won't believe a word you say. And the fact is, I'm just not the kind of girl men fall in love with at first sight.'

'Your mother didn't seem to have any trouble believing me.' Gib watched her scrabbling through the drawers in search of a corkscrew. 'She told me that I sounded like a dream come true,' he went on virtuously.

Phoebe muttered under her breath as she located the corkscrew at last and attacked the foil at the top of the bottle. 'You're not taking this seriously!' she accused him.

'And you're taking it too seriously,' said Gib. 'You need to lighten up, Phoebe! Everything's under control.'

'Easy for you to say,' grumbled Phoebe, twisting the corkscrew. 'Have you organised a suit yet?' She bet he hadn't.

'Yes.'

Oh.

'Well, that's something, I suppose.' The cork popped out and she poured the wine into a glass, pausing for a second to savour its pale golden beauty before she went back to her fretting.

'What about this job you're supposed to have?' she demanded as she carried her glass over to the armchair next to him. 'I've told Mum you're a banker now, so you'd better be able to carry it off.'

'Relax,' said Gib lazily. 'I've been doing some research. Look.' He picked up a brochure from the floor by the sofa and waved it at her.

Phoebe took it with her spare hand. 'This is for the Community Bank,' she said blankly.

'I know.'

'Where did you get it?'

'It was lying on the table with some of the other stuff you brought home with you,' said Gib, and Phoebe was too busy studying the brochure to notice the faint hesitation in his voice. 'I thought I might as well take advantage of the research you've been doing for your programme, so I had a look through it. If anyone asks, I'll say I work in their development section. I ought to be able to bluff my way through on that.'

'That's not a bad idea.' She looked at him with grudging respect. 'It's a bank, but not a real bank.'

'What do you mean, it's not a real bank?' For once Gib was roused out of his lazy good humour and he sat up to object. 'It lends money, it supports its customers, it's an integral part of the financial infrastructure of the countries where it operates...'

Phoebe looked at him in surprise. 'You *have* been reading the brochure, haven't you?'

There was a tiny silence, and then Gib lay back down. 'I told you I'd been doing some research,' he said.

'I'm glad to hear you're getting into your role so well,' she said dryly. 'Anyway, I just meant that because it's an ethical bank, if you meet any other City types there, they won't expect you to be flash and boast about bonuses. They'll probably make allowances if you seem a bit...'

'A bit what?'

'I don't know,' said Phoebe with a touch of irritation. Why did Gib have to pick her up on everything? 'A bit different, I suppose.'

She sipped her wine reflectively, trying to spot the flaws in Gib's idea, but the more she thought about it, the better it seemed. 'No, I think it might work,' she said with gathering excitement. 'We could say that's how we met,' she went on, getting into the idea.

'Exactly,' said Gib.

Phoebe ignored his smugness. 'People know that I've been working on the programme. I'm so desperate that I've asked most of Ben's City friends if they've got any contacts in the States who might know about the Community Bank, but hardly any of them had even heard of it—which is good news for you,' she added as an aside. 'We can pretend that someone put me in touch with you, and you were so impressed by me on the phone that we arranged to meet and... Bam!'

'Ah, so it *was* love at first sight?' said Gib provocatively.

Phoebe rolled her eyes. 'Yes, all right, it was love at first sight, if that's what you want! If you've already told Mum that's how it was, there's not much I can do about it anyway.'

She might be reassured that Gib was getting ready to play his part, but as Ben's wedding approached, Phoebe grew more and more apprehensive. By the time the following Saturday came round, she was so jittery with nerves that she could hardly speak.

'You've got to calm down,' said Bella that morning. 'You're wound so tight, you're going to snap! Here, give me that,' she added, seeing Phoebe lay her dress onto the ironing board. 'You'll just burn it if you try and iron it in that state. Sit down and relax for a minute.'

'I can't relax,' said Phoebe, hugging her arms together edgily as Bella tested the iron with the tip of her finger. 'I keep thinking of all the things that could go wrong.'

'Like what?'

'Like Gib forgetting who he's supposed to be,' she said with a pointed glance at where he sat reading the paper at the table in jeans and a T-shirt, long legs stretched out before him and quite unperturbed by all the activity around him.

'Hey, I resent that!' he said, without looking up from his paper. 'I'm John Gibson, Gib to his friends, development manager at the Community Bank with special responsibility for setting up funding programmes and links between Europe and sub-Saharan Africa, and I can now bore for England *and* the States about development strategies, ethical investment opportunities and interest assessment.'

'See?' said Bella, impressed. 'He'll be fine.'

'I don't know,' said Phoebe fretfully, rummaging through her make-up bag in search of a mirror. 'It would just take one little slip, and they'll all know that my fantastically successful lover is in fact my unemployed lodger!

'I didn't sleep a wink last night thinking about it,' she

went on, opening the mirror and contemplating her face glumly. 'Excellent, bug eyes and puffy skin! Just what I need this morning!'

'Nothing a bit of make-up won't cure,' said Bella reassuringly. 'Put on some lippy and you'll be fine.'

'I think it's going to take more than lipstick this morning,' said Phoebe, refusing to be comforted. 'God, I look a mess!'

'No, you don't,' said Gib, lowering his paper to study her. 'You look absolutely beautiful.'

It was so unexpected that Phoebe's jaw dropped, and Bella looked up from her ironing in surprise.

'Blimey! She hasn't even got her make-up on yet!'

'Phoebe doesn't need make-up. She always looks beautiful to me,' Gib said soulfully, and belatedly Phoebe realised that he was just proving that he had his role down pat.

Mortified by her blush—what if he thought she had taken him seriously?—she lifted her chin and retreated behind her haughtiest air. 'You'd better not say anything like that today, or they'll know you can't be serious,' she said.

'Why?'

Phoebe glanced back at the mirror. Her face stared uncompromisingly back at her. 'I accepted a long time ago that I'm not beautiful, and I never will be,' she said flatly.

Gib looked across the table at her. She wasn't pretty, it was true. Her face was too full of character and her features too strong to be anything as insipid as pretty. Instead she was vivid and dramatic, with those fierce eyes and that mouth that hinted at a passionate nature well hidden behind her prickles.

'I don't agree,' he said.

Phoebe saw Bella's hand still and the sharp look of interest she gave Gib. 'All right, you can drop the act for now,' she said hastily. 'Save it for later, and don't overdo it,' she warned. 'Everyone there has known me for ever, and they know I hate all that gushy lovey-dovey stuff.'

'You might not if you were in love,' said Gib.

'Ben never went in for that kind of thing,' she told him, and he folded his paper and got deliberately to his feet.

'Well, I'm not Ben,' he reminded her, and when Phoebe met his eyes she saw with something of a shock that the familiar laughter was quite gone. 'You're in love with me now, remember?'

Phoebe moistened her lips, wondering why the kitchen was suddenly so airless. 'Just for today,' she managed.

There was an unpleasant silence for a moment, then Gib smiled. It wasn't his usual smile, though. There was something almost grim about it. 'Of course, just for today,' he echoed in a voice empty of expression. He turned for the door. 'Excuse me, I'll go and get ready.'

Phoebe didn't realise that she had been holding her breath until he left and she was able to let it out at last, very carefully. When she glanced back at Bella, she saw that her friend was watching her with a speculative expression.

'I wouldn't push Gib, if I were you,' was all she said, slipping the dress onto its hanger and handing it to Phoebe. 'Here you are. Go and have a shower, and I'll do your make-up for you afterwards.'

'You look fantastic!' she said later when Phoebe was glossed and mascaraed and dusted with Kate's special shimmering powder that promised a radiant golden glow. She made her turn and look at herself in the mirror. In heels and a flame-red suit with a dramatic necklace, Phoebe looked taller and more vivid than ever.

'All you need now is your hat,' said Bella. 'And a smile.'

Phoebe couldn't manage the smile, and wrung her hands together instead. 'Oh, God, Bella, do you think I'm doing the right thing?'

'Yes,' said Bella, who had no time for doubts. 'You're going to be able to go into that wedding with your head held high. Gib will be beside you, and he won't let you down.'

'He'd better not,' said Phoebe tensely.

Bella smoothed the short-sleeved jacket over Phoebe's shoulder. 'He was pretty convincing when he said he thought you were beautiful,' she said, carefully expressionless. 'I wondered how much he was pretending.'

'Of course he was pretending.' Phoebe didn't quite meet her eyes. The last thing she needed was Bella knowing that she had wondered the same for an embarrassing moment or two. 'That's what I'm paying him to do.'

Bella picked up Phoebe's hat. 'You seem to have been getting on better recently,' she commented in the same studiedly casual tone.

'I suppose so,' was all Phoebe would admit.

'I think he really likes you, Phoebe. So does Kate. We think he's just what you need,' she went on when Phoebe could only gape at her.

'No.' Phoebe found her voice at last. 'No, he's not what I need at all.' She shook her head firmly to emphasise the point, although it wasn't clear whether she was trying to convince herself or Bella. 'He's nothing like Ben.'

'Exactly,' said Bella. 'I know you loved Ben, Phoebe, but it's time you moved on. You need someone you can have some fun with, and I can't imagine anyone better than Gib for that.'

'I'm not sure I'm ready to have fun,' Phoebe confessed in a low voice. 'I'm scared of being hurt again, Bella. I don't want to get involved with anyone, let alone Gib. Anyway,' she went on, lifting her chin, 'I think you're wrong about him. Pretending to be in love with me is just a job to him. He was quite happy for me to pay him. He wouldn't be interested in money if he really liked me, would he?'

She needed to remember that, Phoebe told herself as she went downstairs carefully on her high heels.

They found Kate in kitchen, and by the time she had exclaimed over the outfit and heard Bella's account of Gib's unexpected acting ability, Phoebe's nerves were back in full force and her stomach was churning furiously.

She looked at her watch. The ceremony was at two-thirty, and they would need to allow at least two hours to get to the castle. Getting out of London on a Saturday could be a nightmare.

'OK, I've got my bag, got the present, got my hat…what else do I need?'

'Car keys?'

'God, yes, car keys! Where are they?'

Phoebe began scrabbling frantically through the piles of junk on the table. 'I had them yesterday,' she said fretfully. 'I'm sure they're here somewhere. Kate, can you see whether the cat is sitting on them? And where's Gib? We've got to go.'

'I'm here.'

All three girls looked up from where they were burrowing down the sides of the sofa or sifting through the clutter of papers on the worktop, and there was a moment of thunderstruck silence. Kate and Bella frankly stared, and Phoebe froze, breathless as if from a blow.

She couldn't believe how different Gib looked. He had showered and shaved, and changed into a beautifully cut grey suit with a classic white shirt and a pale grey tie. He looked much older, much more respectable, even distinguished, but his sudden grin at their expressions was exactly the same as before.

'Well!' whistled Bella, the first to recover. 'Who'd have thought you'd brush up so nicely!'

Kate walked round him critically. 'Ten out of ten!' she agreed. 'There's just something about a man in a suit, isn't there? What do you reckon, Phoebe? Will he pass?'

Why couldn't she be as easy with him as Kate and Bella were? Gripped by a ridiculous shyness, Phoebe couldn't meet Gib's eyes.

'He looks fine,' she said curtly.

'Are we ready to go?' His voice was warm with that unsettling undercurrent of laughter, so much so that Phoebe began to wonder if she had imagined the formidable look she had glimpsed earlier.

'When I've found my car keys,' she snapped.

'Here.'

To Phoebe's annoyance, Gib spotted them immediately on the sideboard and dangled them from his finger. Snatching them from him, she stalked out to the car, her exit only marred by the fact that she forgot to pick up her hat and her overnight bag.

'Are you OK to drive?' Gib asked when she had stowed them in the boot of her old Peugeot.

'Of course I am.' Phoebe bridled as she opened the driver's door. 'Why shouldn't I be?'

'You seem a bit...tense,' he said carefully.

'Of course I'm tense! I'm going to watch the man I love marrying someone else while lying to my family and friends about having a relationship with my unemployed lodger who's pretending to be a hotshot businessman, and knowing that if anyone even suspects what I'm doing it'll ruin the whole day for everyone!'

And that was quite apart from knowing that her friends thought she should get involved with a man who was only pretending to be nice because she was paying him.

Suddenly Phoebe felt close to tears.

'That's what I meant,' said Gib. 'I know it's going to be difficult for you today. If you want to drive, that's fine by me, but if you want one less thing to think about, I thought it would be something I could do for you.'

Phoebe hesitated, chewing her lip. She didn't want to give in, but she knew that Gib was right. She wasn't in a fit state to drive, and an accident was the last thing she needed right now. Usually, she loved being driven, but she wasn't sure she trusted Gib. He looked like the kind of man who burned along the highways in an open-topped sports car, one hand on the steering wheel and the other on a blonde, not one who would drive her old banger safely and sedately down to Wiltshire.

Gib came round the front of the car to her door. 'You're not really intending to drive in those, are you?' he said, nodding down at her strappy shoes with their delicate heels.

Of course she couldn't drive in them. She could dig out her driving shoes from the boot…or she could just let Gib drive.

Reading the decision in her face, Gib held out his hand and Phoebe put the keys into his outstretched palm.

'As long as you drive carefully,' she said with a flash of her old self as she got into the passenger seat.

Gib inserted the key into the ignition and pushed back the seat to allow room for his longer legs. 'You don't trust me, do you?' he said as he pulled out into the street.

'If I didn't trust you, I wouldn't be exposing you to my family,' said Phoebe, grabbing at the door as a taxi swerved in front of them.

'If you trusted me, you wouldn't be sitting there clutching the door and jamming your foot on an imaginary brake,' said Gib in a dry voice. 'If you're going to do that all the way to Wiltshire I'd rather you drove after all!'

Phoebe made a conscious effort to relax. 'Sorry,' she muttered.

Contrary to all her expectations, Gib was a calm, competent driver, quite unflustered by the London traffic. It was odd seeing him in the driving seat, his hands sure on her steering wheel. Phoebe's eyes kept sliding sideways, and every time the sight of him was like a tiny shock that made her look quickly away.

For a while the conversation was limited to Phoebe's attempts to direct Gib through the labyrinth of back streets to get out onto the M4, but once they hit the motorway, he put his foot down and settled back comfortably into his seat with a wriggle of his shoulders that sent a peculiar little shiver down her spine.

'Do you want to fill me in on a bit more background before we get there?' he said with a sideways glance. 'I know the situation with Ben, and I've got the job covered, but am I likely to meet anyone else I should know about?'

Phoebe looked out of the window at the speeding traffic. 'There'll be various friends who knew me when Ben and I were together, but I suppose we could say that our relationship is too new for me to have mentioned them to you.'

'Ah, yes,' said Gib with a wicked smile. 'When you're as much in love as we are, you've got better things to think about, haven't you?'

Faint colour touched Phoebe's cheekbones. 'Exactly.'

'So it'll just be your family I really need to worry about?'

'Yes.' Phoebe was glad of the chance to move onto a safer topic. 'Mum and Dad are pretty much what you'd expect, and my little sister will be there, too. Lara's the baby of the family. She looks like butter wouldn't melt in her mouth, but don't be fooled. She's sharp as a tack.'

'What does she do?'

'Drives my parents to distraction mostly,' she said wryly.

'She's incredibly bright, but she gets bored so easily. She keeps starting courses and not finishing them, or walking out of perfectly good jobs, and she's always got some unsuitable boyfriend in tow.'

'Not like big sister, then?' said Gib with another of those disconcertingly blue glances.

'No, I'm the boring one of the family.' Phoebe gave an unconscious sigh as she stared through the windscreen and thought about her sister. 'I've had such a conventional life. Fell in love with the boy next door, got a degree, saddled myself with a mortgage... Giving up my job to work for Purple Parrot Productions is the riskiest thing I've ever done, and that's not exactly living dangerously, is it?'

'Is that what you'd like? To live dangerously?'

'Sometimes,' she admitted, 'but I don't think I'd be very good at it. I'm too sensible.'

That was what Ben had said. *You're so sensible, Phoebe. I know that you'll understand that it's not that I don't care for you. It's just that we know each other so well that things aren't that exciting, are they? We can't surprise each other any more.*

'I wish I could be more like Lara sometimes,' she told Gib, pushing away the memory. If she had been, maybe Ben wouldn't have fallen in love with Lisa, who wasn't predictable and familiar. 'She decides she wants to do something, and she does it. She'll try anything. She doesn't stop to think about the consequences, or what might happen if something goes wrong, she just goes for it.'

Gib slid her another glance. 'I'll look forward to meeting her.'

'You'll like her.'

Phoebe was conscious of a faint wistfulness. Her sister had exactly the same streak of recklessness that seemed so much part of Gib. It didn't matter that he was rattling along in the slow lane in her battered old car, or that he was dressed in the most conventional of grey suits, he still exuded an air of danger and excitement that alarmed and intrigued her in equal measure.

Gib would find a kindred spirit in Lara, she thought. Lara was reckless and funny and open, the complete opposite of her big sister in fact.

CHAPTER FIVE

WITHOUT meaning to, Phoebe sighed.

'What's the matter?' Gib was watching her more closely than she realised.

'Nothing,' said Phoebe quickly.

She could feel his blue gaze sharpen assessingly as it rested on her averted profile, but after a moment he evidently decided to let it go.

'OK,' he said. 'What about us?'

'What *about* us?'

'We ought to agree on how we met,' he suggested.

'I thought we'd already decided that.' Phoebe pulled herself together. 'We met when I contacted you about the programme we're making.'

'You don't think that sounds a bit dry?' said Gib. 'I mean, won't they want to know a few more details?'

'Like what?'

'I don't know,' he said, lifting one hand from the steering wheel to gesture vaguely. 'Like whether it was love at first sight for both of us, or did I have to work really hard to win you?'

'Oh, that last one, I think,' said Phoebe crisply. 'I don't want to be a pushover.'

Gib cast her a wry look. 'I can't imagine you ever being that,' he said. 'Still, you obviously didn't play *too* hard to get since I've moved in with you already. In fact,' he went on with one of his swift, sidelong grins, 'I think you'd better just admit it! You couldn't resist me, could you?'

She hated his habit of being right about things like that.

It *would* sound odd if she was claiming to be keeping her distance when Gib had apparently moved into her house barely a week after she had supposedly met him.

'I suppose we'd better say I was swept off my feet,' she agreed stiffly.

Gib's eyes rested thoughtfully for a moment on her averted profile before he looked back at the road. 'What would it take to do that, Phoebe?' he asked.

'I don't know,' she said. 'It's never happened to me. I always knew I loved Ben, so it wasn't something that happened overnight. I can't imagine ever doing anything as rash as falling in love with someone I don't really know,' she admitted. 'I mean, being swept off your feet is all very well in theory, but in practice, how would you be able to trust a man who overwhelmed you and persuaded you into changing your life before you'd had a chance to think about what you were really doing?'

'I thought you wanted to live dangerously?'

'Not that dangerously,' said Phoebe. 'Falling in love like that seems like a sure way to get yourself hurt.'

Gib signalled and then moved out to overtake. 'I think if you fell in love you might change your mind. If you really loved someone, you'd be prepared to take that risk.'

'I've been in love,' she said flatly. 'I took that risk, and I got hurt. I'm not going through that again.'

There was silence for a while. Gib concentrated on driving, and Phoebe looked out of the side window and thought about Ben and the look in his eyes when he had told her that he had fallen in love with Lisa. He was the last person she had ever expected to hurt her. They had been so comfortable together, so gentle, so *safe*. She had thought that was what he had wanted too, but she had been wrong. Perhaps she hadn't known him as well as she had thought.

And then for some reason she found herself remembering

what she had said to Bella about Gib. It would be hard to find a man more different from Ben. Safe was the last word you would use about him! Phoebe could imagine *him* sweeping a girl off her feet all right. He was the type who saw what he wanted and went for it, and if what he wanted was you, you would have little choice in the matter, she thought with a tiny shiver. He would turn your life upside down, spin you around, subject you to a roller coaster of adrenalin and excitement—and then drop you back down to earth with a thump when he was bored and wanted to move on.

No, thank you, thought Phoebe. She could do without that kind of excitement. Living dangerously like that would not be worth the pain and humiliation you would have to endure afterwards. She had had enough of both of *them* in the last year.

'What shall I call you?' Gib broke the silence at last, and she turned to look at him in surprise.

'What's wrong with my name?'

'I was thinking more along the lines of endearments. Do you want to be "darling" or "honey" or what?'

Phoebe grimaced. 'I'm not really a "darling" kind of girl.'

'Why not?'

'Because darlings are soft and sweet and pretty, not sharp and intimidating.'

'Hey,' said Gib with a grin, 'you don't intimidate me, baby!'

She shot him a look. 'I'm not a "baby" either!'

'Shall I call you bunnikins then?'

'Not unless you want to spend the next month with your jaw wired,' said Phoebe evenly, and he threw back his head and laughed.

'But we're so in love!' he pretended to protest.

'We're not that in love,' she said, more unnerved than she wanted to admit by the way Gib looked when he laughed like that. He had obviously taken advantage of American dentistry because his teeth were very white and strong, and the creases starring his eyes deepened in what was—OK, she was prepared to concede this—a disturbingly attractive way. The sound of his laughter rolled around the car and seemed to linger, reverberating over her skin so that she shivered slightly.

If only he wasn't quite so overwhelming. He was so vivid, so vital, that she was left feeling pale and drab and somehow vulnerable in comparison.

Gib was still talking. 'I thought I was supposed to be the perfect man for you?'

'Exactly,' said Phoebe, pulling herself together with an effort. She really must get a grip. 'And everyone knows that I wouldn't let a man who would even *think* about calling me bunnikins within a mile of me!'

'So if they heard me calling you bunnikins, they'd know it had to be true love,' he pointed out.

'Listen, who's paying you here?' she said crossly, feeling herself being drawn into a ridiculous argument that would, on past form, end with her not only agreeing but begging Gib to call her bunnikins. That was how she had ended up in this mess in the first place! She had been determined not to be talked into asking him to act as her imaginary lover, but somehow, here she was, heading down the motorway towards the wedding with Gib beside her.

'If I hear the word bunnikins cross your lips, I'll cut that fee we agreed in half, so don't say I didn't warn you!'

'OK, bunni-boss!'

'Very funny,' she said with a frosty look.

'Perhaps I just call you madam and be done with it, if

you're going to be that stand-offish,' said Gib, pretending to sound aggrieved.

Phoebe gritted her teeth. 'Look, I don't care what you call me, as long as it's not bunnikins, all right? You're supposed to be perfect!'

'If I'm so perfect, how are you going to explain the fact that our fantastic, perfect relationship is going to end shortly after this wedding?'

'Well, I haven't quite decided yet,' she admitted. 'Perhaps I'll discover that you've got a deep dark secret. Everyone knows that I could never love a man who lied to me.'

'Oh?' he said carefully. 'Why's that?'

'I've always had a thing about lying. I hate it.'

'But you lie,' Gib pointed out with a cool glance. 'You've lied to your mother about our relationship and you're going to carry on lying today.'

'That's different,' she protested.

'How?'

'My lies aren't going to hurt anyone.'

'Things aren't always as straightforward as you want them to be,' said Gib, choosing his words with care. 'Sometimes the truth can hurt as much as a lie.'

Did he think she didn't know that? Phoebe thought about Ben, insisting on telling her about Lisa as soon as he knew that he was in love. That was one thing about Ben, he was always absolutely honest. He had never pretended, and if the truth had been unbearably painful, at least it had been better than discovering it from someone else much later.

Gib glanced sideways. Phoebe's face was sad and he cursed himself inwardly for triggering what were obviously unhappy memories. He was supposed to be supporting her today like the good friend he was trying to prove that he was, not making her even more miserable.

'So the idea is that in a couple of weeks' time you're

going to tell your mother that I lied to you and dump me without hearing my side of the story, is that right?' he said, deliberately keeping his voice light and upbeat.

'I'll probably have found out by then that there are lots of other things about you that have begun to irritate me,' said Phoebe loftily, but Gib saw the effort it cost her to reply in kind. 'Your lies will just be the final straw.'

'Wouldn't it be simpler to forget about the whole lies thing?' said Gib. 'Why don't you just say that I'm a bastard who's dumped you?'

'Because I've already been dumped once,' she said with a slight edge to her voice. 'This time I'm the one who gets to do the dumping. And what's more,' she went on, pointing at him for emphasis, '*you* are going to devastated! I'm going to tell Mum that you're making a real nuisance of yourself, sending me flowers every day, showering me with diamonds, and ringing up every five minutes to beg me to give you another chance.'

That was better. Gib pretended to look disconsolate. 'If I'm going to humiliate myself to that extent, I think you should give me one.'

'No way!' Phoebe shook her head definitely and he heaved a sigh.

'You're a hard-hearted woman!'

'You deceived me,' she pointed out.

'Yes, but I couldn't help myself,' said Gib. 'You drive me crazy. I haven't been able to think of anyone but you since I met you.'

Primming her mouth, she tried hard not to laugh. 'You should have thought of that before you abandoned your wife and six children in the States, shouldn't you?'

'Six children? Cut me a break! Wouldn't two be enough?'

'Nope. You've got six little darlings depending on you.'

There was a twitch at the corner of Gib's mouth. 'I'm

surprised I'm in any state for a passionate affair with you in that case! I must be quite a guy!'

'No, you're not,' said Phoebe firmly, realising with an odd start that she was actually enjoying herself. 'It turns out that you're a low, treacherous, lying creep.'

He considered the matter, but after a moment shook his head. 'I don't think that's going to work,' he decided.

'Why not?'

'I don't believe that you would ever be taken in by someone with so little integrity,' he said coolly. 'You're too...' He stopped, searching for the right word.

Too *what*? Phoebe found herself wanting to know, when really she shouldn't be caring one way or another what he thought.

'...too perceptive?' Gib wondered, almost as if she had asked out loud. 'Too honest? Too intelligent, maybe? Anyway, I can't see it happening.'

Hhmmnn. How was she supposed to take *that*? On the surface, being thought intelligent and honest and perceptive ought to be a compliment, but as usual it was impossible to tell from Gib's voice whether he was being serious or not.

In the end, Phoebe chose to ignore his comment altogether. 'All right, maybe there's some ex-girlfriend you forgot to mention,' she offered as an alternative. 'She gets in touch with me, weeping and wailing and complaining that you've broken her heart, and I feel so sorry for her that I break it all off with you.'

Gib lifted an eyebrow. 'Would you really do that?'

'I might if you were annoying me anyway and I was looking for an excuse to end the relationship.'

That disconcerting crease was back at the corner of his mouth. 'But what could I possibly do that would annoy you enough to kick out a man like me—wealthy, successful, a passionate lover—on the say-so of some neurotic ex?' he asked, assuming an aggrieved air.

Phoebe tried to think of all the ways he irritated her, but it was hard to put her finger on exactly why she found him so unsettling. It wasn't so much anything he *did*, she realised. It was just the way he was.

'You're too possessive,' she offered eventually.

'Oh, come on, you'll have to do better than that!'

'And you snore.'

Gib's expression showed how much he thought of that suggestion.

'You don't get on with Kate and Bella.'

He snorted. 'No one's going to believe *that*! I can't imagine anyone not getting on with those two.'

It was true, Phoebe thought, startled by the pang of envy that shot through her. Everybody loved her friends. They were bright and bubbly and fun in a way she could never quite manage. Of course Gib got on with them. It would be a lot easier for him to pretend to be in love with Bella or with Kate than her with her prickles and her sharp tongue.

Still, it was too late to start being sweet now. 'If you're going to be difficult about it, I'll tell everyone I was just using you as a sex toy and got bored with your technique,' she said crisply.

'Ouch!' Gib winced. 'I think I'll take the vengeful girlfriend, thanks!'

He glanced at Phoebe, who was sitting straight in her seat, her fine cheekbones tinged with colour and the smooth dark hair slipping silkily around her face. As he watched, she hooked a swathe behind her ear and he glimpsed the pulse beating nervously in her throat before he made himself look back at the road. She was trying hard, but she must be dreading the day ahead.

'Of course, you realise that *she'll* turn out to be the one who's lying, don't you?' he said, wanting to distract her, to stop her thinking about Ben and the fact that another bride was going to be standing in the place that should have been hers. 'You'll find that out too late, though, and realise that I was perfect after all, and then you'll be sorry!'

'Hah! I am *so* not going to have any regrets,' said Phoebe, shaking back her hair, but Gib was glad to see that she was laughing.

His tomfoolery had diverted her and for the first time she felt able to relax. For a while they talked easily, and it was only when they turned off the motorway that the butterflies started to swoop and flutter around her stomach once more.

Smoothing the map nervously over her knees, Phoebe directed Gib through the lush Wiltshire countryside with one part of her mind, while the other was fully occupied reviewing all the potentially disastrous scenarios that might unfold when they arrived.

'You won't forget that you're going back to London tonight, will you?' she fretted.

'What, and miss that meeting in Zurich? Impossible!'

Phoebe was too dithery by this stage to pick him up on his sarcasm. 'Right, so we'd better order a taxi to the station when we get there. It can pick you up after the reception. If we say half past six, that ought to be fine—oh, next on the left!'

Gib muttered under his breath at the lateness of the instruction and swung the car round the bend with a squeal of tires. 'Thanks for the warning! Do you think you could concentrate on the map and forget how you're going to get rid of me for the moment?'

'Yes, sorry…' Phoebe bent her head diligently over the map, only to be struck by another thought. Gib looked so much the part in his suit that it was easy to forget that he didn't have a real job. She chewed her lip, eyeing him under her lashes.

'Um…have you got enough cash to get you back to London?' she asked awkwardly. 'I brought some extra with me, just in case, so if you need it…'

Gib's smile twisted as she trailed off uncomfortably. 'Don't worry about it,' he said. 'I'll be fine.'

'I don't want you to be out of pocket.'

'I tell you what,' he said briskly. 'I'll keep an account of everything I spend today and we can tally it up at the end. You can add it to the fee we agreed.'

Phoebe went back to her map-reading. 'Oh. Right. Yes, of course. If you're happy with that.'

Now that the subject had come up, perhaps it might be an idea to sort out a few other things, she thought. Things she had deliberately avoided thinking about so far.

She cleared her throat. 'Maybe we should talk about what happens when we get there,' she said stiltedly. 'Lay down a few rules of engagement, so to speak.'

'Engagement?' Gib lifted his brows. 'I thought we were just lovers?'

'Engagement as in a battle,' she said with a frosty look. As if he didn't know.

'Battle? I didn't know things were going to get that serious,' he said, not bothering to disguise the undercurrent of laughter in his voice. 'Perhaps I should have negotiated danger money?'

'You might think so after today,' said Phoebe, unamused. 'I should warn you that you are going to be kissed a lot by people like my mother and Penelope who are going to fall on your neck for rescuing me from dreary spinsterhood.'

'I don't mind a few kisses,' he said equably.

'Good.' Phoebe bit her lip. 'And, er, I might have

to…you know…hold your hand or something. Just for show,' she added hastily.

'Holding hands, eh?' said Gib. 'Passionate stuff!'

'Nobody's going to expect you to throw me down and ravish me in front of the bridesmaids just to prove your affection,' she retorted in a tart voice. 'You're back in England now!'

'Still, I think we could do a bit better than holding hands,' he said, amused. 'Maybe we could go wild and have a little kiss every now and then, just to show them how much in love we are?'

Phoebe's colour deepened. She wished she could treat it as lightly as Gib. It was all just a big joke to him. 'If you don't mind,' she said stiffly.

Gib slid her one of those unsettling sideways looks. 'No, I don't mind,' he said.

'Just so long as you realise that it doesn't mean anything if…if…'

'If you kiss me back?'

'Yes,' she said, grateful to him for putting it into words but obscurely resentful of his casual attitude. He might at least *pretend* to find the prospect of kissing each other as awkward as she did!

She would just have to convince him that she was equally businesslike about the whole affair, Phoebe decided. 'So that's the first rule of engagement for today,' she said briskly. 'No getting involved, or misinterpreting any form of physical contact that we may have today.'

'Fair enough,' said Gib with a slight smile. 'What's the second rule?'

Good question. Phoebe wracked her brains for something suitable. 'Stick to the story we've agreed, and keep it simple.'

'And the third?'

'Two rules is quite enough,' she said a little crossly. She couldn't think up any more.

'OK,' he said. 'I should be able to remember those.'

'You'd better,' said Phoebe, rather proud of her rules now that she came to think of them. She had made it clear that their relationship today was to be a purely businesslike one, and ensured that there would be no misunderstandings between them. How cool could you get?

Even so, as they left the main road and cut across country towards the castle, she found herself fiddling with the map on her knees, turning over the corner until it was dog-eared and tatty.

Gib glanced at her. 'Nervous?'

'Yes.' What was the use of pretending, after all? 'Terrified might be a better word, if you really want to know!'

'What's the worst that could happen?' he asked, wanting to make her feel better but not sure how. Weren't friends supposed to know this kind of thing instinctively?

Phoebe was still mangling the page between her fingers. 'I suppose that we won't seem convincing together,' she said eventually. 'People like my sister pick up on body language. They'll be watching us so closely, I'm afraid they'll see that…you know…that we aren't really lovers.'

'You mean they'll be able to tell just from looking at us that we haven't even kissed?'

'Well…yes.'

Gib checked his mirror before pulling over into the entrance to a farm gate. This was one thing he *could* do to help her. 'Let's kiss now, then,' he said as he put on the handbrake and switched off the ignition.

'*What?*'

Calmly, he unclipped his seat belt and reached across to undo hers. 'You're the one who's worried people are going to guess that we haven't kissed,' he pointed out reasonably. 'If we kiss now, they won't be able to do that, will they?'

'You're not serious!' Astounded, Phoebe struggled to sit up straight, but that only brought her closer to him as he leaned over towards her, so she hastily retreated, shrinking back into her seat.

Gib paused. 'Don't you think it's a good idea?' he asked. 'Personally, I think it would be easier to kiss you for the first time when there are just two of us and not in front of an entire wedding reception, but it's up to you,' he said, as casually as if they were discussing whether or not to stop for a coffee. 'Of course,' he added with a look at Phoebe's face, 'if you don't want to, that's fine. I don't want to force you. I just thought it might help.'

'No…no,' she said, abruptly changing her mind as he made to sit back. 'You might have a point there.'

The idea of a first kiss under the interested gaze of assorted family and friends had been enough to make Phoebe blench. Ben might be watching too, and if anyone would be able to tell that she and Gib had never kissed before, he would. No, Gib was right. It was far better to have a go here. At least then she would know what to expect.

'No,' she said a little breathlessly. 'Let's do it.'

'OK.'

'OK,' Phoebe agreed, moistening her lips nervously.

Gib was disconcerted to discover just how much he wanted to kiss her. Of course, kissing like this wasn't really what friends did, he reminded himself, and a friend was all he was supposed to be. On the other hand, pretending to be Phoebe's lover was just a way of helping her out, so he was *being* a friend. A kiss under these circumstances wouldn't really count, would it? And it wasn't even as if it would be a real kiss, he reminded himself, remembering her rules of engagement. Surely even Josh couldn't object?

Lifting his hand, he pushed the silky hair away from her face. The green eyes staring back at him were wide and distinctly wary, in spite of her decision.

Gib smiled. 'Relax,' he said. 'Think of it as a dress rehearsal.'

He laid his palm against her soft cheek and tipped her chin up with his thumb. Then, very slowly so as not to alarm her, he touched his mouth to hers.

The feel of his warm, firm lips sent a jolt through Phoebe. She had been bracing herself against his touch, but when it came she was still unprepared for the clutch of her heart or the wash of sheer pleasure that lapped along her veins.

It was just pretending, of course. Gib was right, this was only a practice. Still, it did feel nice, she thought hazily. It felt very nice, so much so, in fact, that when his fingers slid into her hair and his kiss deepened persuasively she didn't try to resist. Instead, she let him push her back into the seat and kissed him back, her lips parting eagerly and her arms winding around his neck, enjoying the tightness of his hands in her hair, holding her still, enjoying the taste of his mouth and the feel of his hard body pressing against hers. Oh, yes, it was very, very nice...

And then, somehow, nice wasn't the word. Something indefinable changed, banishing niceness, as their kisses became hungrier and more demanding. Lost in the pounding of her heart and the surge of sensation, Phoebe was half-intoxicated, half-scared by the heat flaring between them. It was darkly, secretly exciting, it was dangerously intoxicating, it was much, much more than nice, and it was out of control.

This isn't what they were supposed to be practising, the thought drifted elusively through Phoebe's mind, but she was too far gone to care, and it was only when Gib broke the kiss reluctantly that her brain cleared enough for her to think that it shouldn't have been like that at all. It should have been a chaste little peck on the lips not...not *that*.

For a long, long moment they could only stare at each other, both breathing raggedly. Gib's eyes were very blue, their mocking gleam for once entirely absent.

Phoebe's heart was jerking frantically. She couldn't have spoken if she had tried. She could only think how close he still was and how easy it would be for them to kiss again. The same knowledge was reflected in Gib's eyes, and the possibility shimmered tantalisingly in the air between them until he pushed himself abruptly away with a muttered exclamation.

Raking his fingers through his hair, he sat back in the driving seat. 'Well,' was all he could say.

'Well,' Phoebe agreed unsteadily.

'I'm glad we didn't do that in front of your parents.'

'God, yes,' she said, appalled at the very thought.

Gib ran a hand over his face and tried to calm his pounding heart. So much for kissing her like a friend! But how had he been supposed to know how warm and exciting and *right* she would feel? How hard it would be to let her go?

'Sorry, I got a bit carried away,' he said after a moment.

'It's all right.' Phoebe drew a shaky breath. She mustn't let him see how that kiss had affected her. 'Lucky we agreed that first rule of engagement, isn't it?' she said, trying for bright, breezy unconcern but failing utterly to carry it off.

Gib didn't look at her. 'Very lucky,' he agreed dryly.

There was another uncomfortable silence.

Phoebe concentrated on breathing—in, out, in, out—until the deafening boom of her pulse receded and she was able to risk a glance at Gib, hoping to see that he was in a similar state. Of course, that *would* be the moment he looked at her, and to her annoyance he looked exactly the same as he always did. The lurking laughter was back in the blue eyes, as if they had never held that disturbing expression, as if they had not stared wordlessly into hers barely moments ago. Phoebe could almost believe that she had imagined the way they looked then.

'You've got lipstick on the corner of your mouth,' she said, surprised at how steady her voice sounded.

He wiped casually at his mouth with his thumb. 'Better?'

'Yes.' She twisted the driving mirror round to face her and made an attempt to repair her lipstick, hoping he wouldn't notice how her hands were shaking.

He did, of course.

'Are you OK?' he asked in concern.

Phoebe snapped the top back on her lipstick and summoned a brilliant smile. 'I'm fine,' she lied. 'Absolutely fine.'

When they pulled up in the courtyard, a number of wedding guests were milling around by the great doorway to the castle, brushing cheeks and clashing hats together as they caught up with old acquaintances.

Gib switched off the engine.

The silence in the car was very loud. Phoebe didn't move. For the last few miles she had been so preoccupied with trying not to think about that shattering kiss, and failing utterly, that she had forgotten to worry about the wedding. Now the full realisation of just how completely she was going to lie to her family and her friends hit her and she sat staring rigidly ahead, consumed by panic.

'Phoebe?'

'This is crazy,' she said, swallowing nervously. 'I'm terrified of getting out of the car and meeting my own family and people I've known and loved for years!'

For answer, Gib got out of the car and put on his jacket. He wasn't going to think about that kiss any more. He was

Phoebe's friend, not her lover, and he was going to see her through this. Straightening his tie, he collected Phoebe's hat from the boot and came round to open her door so that she had little choice but to swing her legs out and stand up.

'Now, listen,' he said, setting the hat on her head, 'it's going to be great. You're going to keep everyone happy and save your own face by getting through this day with your head held high. I think you're brave and you're beautiful, so get in there and knock 'em dead.'

Phoebe looked into his face and saw that the blue eyes were serious again, just as they had been after he kissed her, and for a moment she felt quite giddy with the memory of what it had felt like.

'I'll be right beside you,' said Gib, and suddenly it was easy for her to square her shoulders and walk across towards the others.

'Smile,' he murmured under his breath, and Phoebe, who had been thinking about the light touch of his hand against her back, quickly pasted on a smile.

Just in time, too.

'Phoebe!'

Lara spotted her first, and came running over to hug her. 'You look fantastic!' she exclaimed.

Very aware of how many pairs of eyes had swivelled in her direction at the sound of her name, Phoebe hugged her sister back. 'Thank you,' she said. 'You don't look so bad yourself!'

'I don't have that extra glow that comes from being in love!' said Lara, turning to smile at Gib with frank curiosity. 'You must be Gib,' she said. 'We've all been dying to meet you!'

In spite of herself, Phoebe tensed and a faint colour tinged her cheeks. Her sister had never been anything but totally upfront. 'This is my sister, Lara,' she said, a little disturbed to find that she was jealous of the appreciative smile Gib gave Lara and the easy way they hugged as if they had known each other for ever.

They were so alike, she thought with a pang. Both completely irresponsible, both blessed with that carefree charm that carried them through life. It was obvious already that they were going to get on like a house on fire.

And yes, there was Lara tucking her hand through his arm as if she owned him. 'Come and meet Mum and Dad. I know they can't wait to see you.'

Gib held out his free hand to Phoebe as if it was the most natural thing in the world, and she was alarmed at how comforting she found his warm grip as Lara led them through the crowd, talking excitedly. In fact, she rather missed it when he released her to let her kiss her parents.

Her mother had obviously been on the lookout for them, as she dragged her father over to meet them halfway. Phoebe made the introductions nervously, but she needn't have worried. Gib judged the handshake with her father perfectly and let her mother kiss him enthusiastically.

'We're all *so* pleased you could come,' she said. 'Phoebe told us how busy you are at the moment.'

Fortunately there was no time for much more as the guests were starting to drift towards the room where the ceremony would be held, but Phoebe knew her mother would be planning a detailed interrogation later. She just hoped Gib would be able to keep up the pretence under *real* pressure!

CHAPTER SIX

WELL, if he couldn't, there wasn't much she could do about it now, she realised. A certain fatalism crept over Phoebe. It was too late to change her mind, and confess that she had invented herself a lover. That would really spoil everyone's day, hers most of all.

And she had to admit that Gib was doing a great job so far, being amusing without being too pushy. Her mother was obviously charmed, and Phoebe could tell that her father was impressed too, which surprised her. With his military background, she would have expected Gib to be exactly the type to set his moustache bristling.

Perhaps it was the suit? Gib certainly looked different today. Phoebe studied him surreptitiously as they made their way into a charming circular tower room. It was hard to believe this was the same irritating man who lazed around her kitchen all day. He looked broader, and more solid somehow, and while the suit might be conventional it would take more than that to make him look like the serious, sensible men her father approved of. His face was too mobile, his eyes too full of laughter, his mouth too ready to twitch into a smile. Even straight faced, there was a daredevil quality about him, a reckless edge that set him apart from all the other identically dressed men in the room. Phoebe was amazed that her father couldn't see it.

Lara was beckoning, and Phoebe and Gib edged past others in the row to sit next to her.

'Are you OK?' Lara whispered to her.

'I'm fine,' said Phoebe. 'Why?'

Lara nodded towards the front of the room where the groom was waiting nervously with his best man. 'I was afraid it might be difficult for you seeing Ben again,' she explained tentatively.

Ben. Phoebe stared at him, confused. He was the love of her life, her soul mate, the man she had dreamed of marrying as long as she could remember. Shouldn't she have noticed him as soon as she came in?

She shook her head a little as if to clear it. This was the moment she had been dreading for months. She couldn't believe that his presence hadn't even registered with her until Lara had pointed him out. Something was wrong somewhere, surely?

'No...no, I'm fine,' she said again to Lara, but she didn't feel fine really. She felt disorientated and unnerved, as if the one certain thing in her life had suddenly vanished.

'I'm not surprised,' Lara whispered back. 'I'd be fine if I had a man like Gib,' she added enviously. 'He's a bit gorgeous, isn't he?'

Involuntarily, Phoebe's eyes returned to Gib on her other side. He was talking to a couple on his left, and making the girl giggle. His head was turned away so that all she could see of his face was the lean line of his jaw, but her heart dipped and lurched anyway. She swallowed.

'He's all right,' she said, knowing that Lara wouldn't expect her to gush, but her sister only laughed.

'You're not fooling anyone, Phoebe! It's obvious you can't keep your eyes off him.'

After that, of course, Phoebe tried everything not to look at Gib again, but it was impossible when she was sitting right next to him. She tried to concentrate on the ceremony, but no matter how fiercely she stared ahead, her eyes kept drifting sideways, distracted by ridiculous details, like the length of his thigh, or the whiteness of his collar against his

brown skin, or the laughter lines fanning the corner of his
eyes, and the memory of how it had felt to kiss him flared
along her veins all over again.

Once, Gib caught her looking at him. His eyebrow lifted
in a faint question, obviously wondering why she kept staring at him. Terrified in case he thought that she had already
forgotten their first rule of engagement and was reading
more into that kiss than the practice it had been, Phoebe
jerked her gaze away so abruptly that her dark hair swung
beneath her hat.

At the front of the room, Ben and Lisa were about to
exchange rings. Shifting upright in her chair, Phoebe's
brows drew together in an effort of concentration. This was
Ben, she reminded herself. Ben, whom she had loved and
wanted as long as she could remember. It had felt so right
and so comfortable to be with him, that she had never imagined that he would be making those vows to somebody else.
She should be thinking about him, not about Gib and the
way they had kissed in the car.

As Ben promised to love and to honour Lisa 'so long as
we both shall live', Phoebe found herself remembering
when he had told her that he would love *her* for ever. They
had been so happy together for so long. Impossible not to
think about the times they had shared or to feel a pang as
she watched him slide the ring onto Lisa's finger.

But it was just a pang. She had dreaded this moment for
months, expecting to feel a terrible, tearing pain in her heart,
not this wistful sadness for the dreams she had nurtured for
so long.

So this was it. Ben was married and there was no way to
turn back the clock. No more pretending that he might,
maybe, change his mind, or that somehow Lisa would disappear and everything would be the way it had been before.
It was time to stop wishing and hoping and dreaming that

things could be different, time to start accepting that she was on her own and making the best of it.

Phoebe wasn't aware of her expression changing, but she suddenly found her hand gathered into Gib's. He held it in a warm, strong clasp that was amazingly comforting, and although she didn't dare look at him, she didn't pull her hand away either. Instead, she watched Ben kiss Lisa and felt Gib's fingers tighten around her own and wondered how it was possible to feel aware of every tiny millimetre of his skin pressed against hers.

The string quartet in the bow-window struck up a suitably celebratory tune and the bride and groom turned, beaming, to their guests, who stirred in anticipation of the champagne to come.

It was over, thought Phoebe, and knew that she ought to feel relieved while feeling only a curious sense of deflation when Gib let go of her hand. People were standing up and pressing forward to congratulate the happy couple, but Lara was already nudging them towards the door.

'Might as well get a head start on the champagne,' she said. 'We can do the kissy-kissy bit later.'

They weren't the only ones to have the same idea, and the walled garden, romantically lined with herbaceous borders and climbing roses, was soon crowded with little groups of guests clutching flutes of champagne and, in the case of the women, trying not to get their heels stuck in the grass.

This was the big test, thought Phoebe, her stomach clenching with nerves again. Gib was going to be exposed to some pretty expert questioners, beginning with her mother, who was making a beeline for them. She would have to stick beside him until she could manoeuvre him over to Ben's tedious uncle, who could be relied upon not to talk about anything but sport, or if things got really bad to

Penelope and Derek's neighbour who was about ninety-seven and unlikely to cross-examine him on the detail of banking or be able to hear much about his supposedly passionate affair with Ben's ex-fiancée.

Not that you could ever tell with old ladies, of course. In Phoebe's experience they were much sharper than they let on, and could hear perfectly well when it suited them.

'Careful,' she said in an undertone as her mother rushed up. 'You're about to be exposed to advanced interrogation techniques. The SAS send soldiers to Mum for practice on withholding information if they're captured by enemy forces, and very few of them pass the test!'

Gib only sent her a glimmering smile before he turned to greet her mother. For a while they chatted easily, and Phoebe could see her mother's smile broadening as she ticked her way through a mental check-list, obviously awarding Gib full points.

Now they had moved on to discuss the wedding. 'It's a beautiful setting,' commented Gib, glancing around him at the battlemented walls with their mullioned windows, spectacular doors and worn old stone.

'Ye-es.' Her mother clearly wasn't convinced. 'Ben and Lisa were very keen on the idea of having the wedding at a castle, but personally I prefer a more traditional setting. I'm hoping Phoebe will choose to have a church wedding.'

'*Mu-um*!' Phoebe shot her an agonised look.

'Oh, don't worry, dear, I'm not hinting,' said her mother airily.

Not much! Phoebe thought bitterly.

'It's just that there's such a pretty church in the village, it seems a shame not to make the most of it.'

'Well, maybe we'll bear that in mind,' said Gib, unable to resist the opportunity of putting an arm around Phoebe. 'What do you think, darling?'

'I think it's too early to be talking about weddings,' she said tightly, acutely aware of his arm around her and of her mother's eyes bulging with interest at that carelessly dropped 'darling' and the even more casual way he had suggested that they were thinking about getting married.

'It's never too early to start making plans,' her mother said eagerly. 'Sometimes you have to book the church months in advance.'

'Yes, well, we're nowhere near that stage yet,' said Phoebe firmly. She tried to move out of the circle of Gib's arm but he held her against him without any apparent effort and, short of an undignified struggle, it looked as if she would have to stay where she was.

She could see her mother's mind already flickering to dresses and flowers and coordinating table arrangements, and hastened to nip the very idea of marriage in the bud before her mother got out a megaphone and announced it to the entire county.

'Now, hold on, Mum,' she said firmly. 'We haven't decided anything definite yet. Have we?' she added to Gib with a look that dared him to contradict her.

Gib met it blandly before turning back to her mother. 'I've asked Phoebe to marry me every day since we met,' he confided. 'She won't give me an answer one way or another, so I'm just going to have to keep on asking until she does.'

'Well, it's not like you to be coy, Phoebe!' said her mother, clearly thrilled.

'I'm not being coy,' snapped Phoebe, shooting a dagger glance at Gib. What had happened to the second rule? Stick to the story and keep it simple: it wasn't *that* hard to remember, was it? Still, in one way she was relieved at the rush of nervous irritation. It was much easier to be cross with Gib than to be burningly aware of him the way she had been since he kissed her. That kiss had seemed a good idea at the time, but Phoebe wasn't so sure now.

'I just think that marriage is an important step,' she told her mother. 'It's not something to rush into.'

'I'm the last person to suggest that it was,' her mother said, bridling. 'But if you know you've found the right person for you, there's no reason to wait, is there? And you don't want to wait too long, dear,' she added with a pointed look.

Phoebe rolled her eyes. 'Go ahead, Mum, why not say it? You're thirty-two, time's running out, beggars can't be choosers?'

'Don't be so silly, Phoebe,' her mother tutted. 'Having a man like Gib want to marry you hardly makes you a beggar! I'm sure there would be thousands of girls who'd be more than happy to have him if you don't want him.'

Gib laughed. 'I don't think so, but even if there were, it wouldn't make any difference to me.' His arm tightened around Phoebe and he smiled down into her indignant face. 'I knew the moment I saw Phoebe that she was the only one for me, and I'm just going to keep on asking her until she gives in.'

Of course, her mother was delighted. 'That's right, don't you listen to her, Gib dear,' she said, patting his arm. 'She's always been so stubborn! She just doesn't know what's good for her sometimes.'

'Mum, I think I see Penelope over there,' said Phoebe through gritted teeth. 'I want her to meet Gib. We'll catch up with you later.'

She practically dragged Gib away. Yes, this was excellent. She really *was* cross with him now. 'I don't know who I want to kill first,' she muttered furiously out of the side of her mouth like a gangster. 'You or my mother!'

Gib was all outraged innocence. 'Why, what have I done?'

'You know perfectly well! All that stuff about getting married!'

'I didn't say that we were getting married. I said that I wanted to marry you.'

'It's the same thing! Now everyone will be on at me to announce our engagement!'

'I was just being creative,' Gib objected. 'I made it obvious that I'm in love with you, and your mother will remember the fact that you were hesitating when you tell her you've dumped me. It'll make you look much better in the end. I thought that was what you wanted.'

'What I *wanted* was for you to do what I'm paying you to do!' snapped Phoebe, only to press the heel of her hand against her forehead a moment later. 'Sorry, sorry, I'm sorry,' she sighed. 'I'm just on edge. I shouldn't have snapped at you. I know you're doing me a favour by coming along today.'

It was Gib's turn to feel guilty. 'No, it's my fault,' he apologised. 'I just thought it would be more convincing if I seemed to be thinking about marriage.'

'Maybe you're right.' Phoebe helped herself to a glass of champagne from a passing waiter and took a gulp. She would need it to get through today! 'We may as well go with the idea that we're getting married now,' she went on, resigned. 'After all, if we can fool Mum, we can fool anyone, and she's bound to tell everyone that we are engaged anyway. She's probably been on to the vicar already, checking out which Saturdays are free!'

Spotting Ben's mother bearing down on them, she gave Gib a nudge. 'Careful now, this is Penelope.'

'Hello, darling.' Penelope enveloped her in a warm embrace before turning with undisguised interest. 'So this is

Gib? We're so glad you could come,' she told him, giving him a hug for good measure. 'We were all thrilled when Sheila told us that Phoebe had met a gorgeous man! She seemed to think it sounded quite serious?'

She looked hopefully between them, and Phoebe bowed to the inevitable.

'Well, we're thinking about following Ben and Lisa's example,' she said. Snuggling against Gib in a suitably besotted pose, she felt his arm close around her with disturbing speed.

Penelope clapped her hands together. 'Oh, that's marvellous news! Your mother must be thrilled! She's been so worried about you.'

'It's just maybe at the moment,' Phoebe stressed. 'We haven't made any definite plans yet,' she hurried on before Gib could jump in and invent a date. She wouldn't put it past him. Left to his own devices, he would no doubt be dressing her up in a meringue and saddling her with a string of little bridesmaids in matching taffeta dresses!

Distracted by someone waving at her behind Phoebe's shoulder, Penelope clicked her tongue in frustration. 'Look, I must go. It's hopeless trying to talk to anyone at this stage, but we'll have a proper chat later tonight. It's just family and close friends staying, and we're all dying for the chance to get to know you properly,' she added, beaming at Gib.

'Oh, Gib won't be here,' Phoebe put in quickly, straightening out of his hold. She had had enough of being winsome. 'He's got to get back to London tonight. In fact, we were just saying he should get the receptionist to book him a taxi, weren't we, Gib?'

'We couldn't talk about anything else,' he agreed.

'Oh, but why?' cried Penelope, looking from one to the other in disappointment and missing the irony in Gib's tone.

Phoebe nudged Gib. 'An important business meeting, I'm afraid,' he said obediently.

'Not on a Sunday, surely?'

'It's first thing on Monday. In Switzerland,' Phoebe added with an edge of desperation. 'So he'll have to fly there tomorrow.'

'Still, it's only a couple of hours to London from here, so even if the flight's at lunchtime, you'd have plenty of time to catch the plane,' Penelope pointed out.

'That's true,' said Gib slowly.

Phoebe stared meaningfully at him. 'What about all the preparation you've got to do?'

'I've done most of that,' he told her with an easy smile. 'I just need to read through a report, and I could do that on the flight.'

'Oh, *do* stay!' Penelope implored him. 'I'm sure it would mean a lot to Phoebe if you were here tonight, and we all want a chance to meet you properly. It's not as if we can't squeeze you in, either,' she added with a twinkling look. 'Phoebe's got a huge room over in the tower, and she'll be rattling around in it all on her own. You'd much rather Gib was with you, wouldn't you, Phoebe?'

What could she say? Phoebe gritted her teeth and managed a smile. 'I just don't want to affect Gib's work. I know he's under a lot of pressure at the moment,' she added with a look that she hoped would remind Gib just what work he was supposed to be doing today.

'You're more important than work,' said Gib, ignoring it completely.

Penelope beamed at him, delighted. 'So you'll stay tonight?'

'Yes, I'd like to. Thanks.'

'Wonderful! Oh, there's Ben.' His mother waved him

over excitedly. 'Look who's here,' she told him, 'and with the most marvellous news!'

Ben had become separated from his bride somewhere in the crowd, so he had to face Phoebe unsupported while his mother bustled happily off. He looked a bit uncomfortable—as well he might, thought Gib sourly as he watched the other man plant an awkward kiss on Phoebe's cheek.

'Thank you for coming,' he told her. 'I hoped you would.'

'Of course I came,' said Phoebe, feeling very poignant as she returned his kiss. Once they had been everything to each other, and now Ben couldn't quite meet her eyes. 'I couldn't miss your wedding.'

Gib watched her narrowly. She was smiling, but he thought he could see a strained look around her eyes and a sadness in her smile. He wanted to punch Ben on the nose and gather her into his arms and make everything better. As it was, all he could do was stand there and watch her being brave.

'I hope you and Lisa will be very happy,' she was saying to Ben. 'I'm sure you will.'

'Thank you,' said Ben, which Gib thought was a bit inadequate. He could at least have acknowledged what a difficult moment this was for Phoebe, or said how much he appreciated her efforts to pretend that everything was absolutely fine and that he hadn't broken her heart.

As it was, the other man looked distinctly ill at ease. Gib studied him, unimpressed. What did Phoebe see in him? He looked pleasant enough, but dull, Gib decided dismissively. Not enough character in his face to deal with Phoebe. She needed someone with a bit more fire to appreciate her.

'This is Gib,' Phoebe introduced him awkwardly, and the two men shook hands without any noticeable enthusiasm.

'Congratulations,' said Gib.

There was a tiny pause. Phoebe kept her smile pinned to

her face and tucked her hand in Gib's arm. 'Congratulate us, too, Ben. Gib and I are thinking about getting married.'

'Really?' Ben looked taken aback for a moment.

Gib could practically see the relief warring with surprise and a touch of chagrin in his face. No doubt Phoebe was supposed to stay broken-hearted for ever, not find someone else.

'That's great news,' Ben recovered, kissing Phoebe again. 'Congratulations, Phoebe.' He looked warily at Gib. 'You're a lucky man.'

'I know,' said Gib discouragingly.

The moment Ben had moved on to greet other well-wishers, Phoebe rounded on Gib. 'Did you have to be quite so unfriendly?' she demanded. She had never seen him behave like that before. For a moment there he had looked quite grim. 'This is Ben's wedding day. You're supposed to be nice to him!'

'You can't expect me to fawn all over the man who hurt the woman I love,' said Gib with a slight edge.

'I don't think there's any need to take your role that seriously! Ben looked as if he were afraid you were about to punch him.'

'It might have livened him up a bit,' Gib beckoned a waiter over and exchanged his empty glass for a full one. 'What do you see in that guy, anyway? He's not exactly a ball of fire, is he?'

'Ben is a very nice man,' said Phoebe defensively. 'He's kind and honest and...and reliable—unlike some people I could mention! Why on earth did you tell Penelope you would spend the night when we had already agreed you would go back to London?'

'Because no self-respecting fiancé would leave you on your own the very night you most need support. Even if you were madly in love with me, it would be hard for you to see Ben getting married, and Penelope obviously knows that. If I'd gone back to London making some lame excuse about flying to Switzerland on Monday it really would have looked suspicious.'

Gib told himself that he was only trying to offer her support. He did think it would be easier for Phoebe if she had a friend with her tonight. He had hated the idea of getting on a train and leaving her to cope on her own. She might not want him, but he thought that she would need someone, and it might as well be him. The fact that he had leapt at the opportunity of staying had absolutely nothing to do with knowing that this might be the only chance he would have to get this close to her.

Of course not.

Phoebe eyed him with some frustration. It *sounded* reasonable enough, and the only argument she could really come up with was that he wasn't doing as he was told, which would come across as a bit childish.

Feeling rattled, she sipped edgily at her champagne. How could she tell Gib that she was far more bothered by the prospect of spending the whole night with him than she had been about coming face to face with Ben? She wasn't even sure that she was ready to admit it to herself.

'It'll certainly look suspicious if you leave now!' she said crossly. 'Then Penelope really would think we'd had a row. I suppose we'll just have to make the best of it.'

Suppressing a sigh, she looked around her, and forced a smile as she caught the eye of an old friend of Ben's family. 'We'd better circulate. From now on, could you *please* not introduce any more variations on the story we agreed? If we get separated, say as little as possible, and when you do, stick to neutral topics. Talk about cricket or something.'

Gib snapped into a mock salute. 'Whatever you say, boss.'

*   *   *

Phoebe picked up a plate and joined the queue for the buffet. Round tables had been set out where the guests could sit down or move around informally, and she looked around as casually as she could, trying to spot Gib, who had drifted from her side in far too relaxed a fashion. She didn't trust him now.

A girl who had known her when she was going out with Ben was standing next to her, rabbiting on about some skiing holiday, but Phoebe was too busy wondering where Gib was and what he was saying to concentrate. She nodded and put in an occasional 'yes' or an 'oh, really?' while her eyes scanned the crowd with increasing nervousness.

There he was! Phoebe's gaze did a double take and swung back to where she had spotted Gib sitting at a table with— oh, God!—her parents and Lara, and they all seemed to be getting on famously.

Typical, she fumed. There must be a hundred strangers here Gib could have picked to sit and make small talk with, but no! He had to choose the three people who were most likely to interrogate him closely and pick up on any weaknesses in their story!

Hastily grabbing a couple of vol-au-vents and a chicken leg, Phoebe muttered an excuse and, leaving Vanessa still yapping about drag lifts and chalet girls, fought her way across the room towards him to try and stop him before he embellished any more aspects of their supposed relationship. It took ages, though, as people kept hailing her, all delighted to see her again and eager to tell her how much they liked Gib.

He was so charming, they told her.

So funny.

So interesting.

'So attractive!' sighed more than one girl enviously. 'You are lucky, Phoebe.'

Hadn't she told Gib very clearly to stick to neutral topics? It didn't sound as if he had listened to a word she had said, Phoebe thought furiously. Far from lurking quietly on the sidelines talking about the weather or the lack of hold-ups on the motorway, he had obviously been in the thick of things, circulating breezily and talking to everyone who knew her!

Smile fixed, she agreed for the umpteenth time that Gib was wonderful and struggled on through the tables to her family.

'Ah, there you are!' her mother waved gaily and Gib turned quickly to see Phoebe suck in her breath to squeeze in between two chairs, holding her plate high to clear the heads. She looked hot and flustered, and beneath her hat he could see that her jaw was gritted and her smile decidedly brittle.

He got to his feet and pulled out a chair for her to sit down beside him. 'I lost you,' he said, taking the plate from her as a precautionary measure. Now that she was close, he could see that her eyes were flashing an unmistakably irate message, and he didn't want vol-au-vents all down his suit. 'I was hoping you'd find me eventually.'

'Gib's been keeping us entertained,' Lara told Phoebe, who was half tempted to refuse to sit next to Gib but couldn't think of a reason that wouldn't make her look childish.

'So I saw,' she said rather grimly instead as she sat down in the chair he still held.

'He's been telling us all about how you met,' Lara went on. 'You never told us it was quite that romantic, Phoebe!'

Romantic? What had he been telling them? Phoebe looked at Gib with foreboding, which only deepened when she saw his eyes dancing. She wished they wouldn't *do* that. It only made her more nervous.

'I didn't tell them *everything*,' he assured her, straight faced, and to Phoebe's consternation her family laughed merrily, as if he had already told them more than enough.

'Perhaps I should know what he *did* tell you,' she said, holding on to her temper with difficulty.

'He said it was a very easy mistake to make.'

'And that it was wonderful to meet someone without any preconceptions about him.'

'Yes, and that one of the reasons he loves you is that you just don't care what he does.'

They beamed at her.

Phoebe looked at Gib. 'Is that right?' she said, unable to think of anything else, other than the obvious option which was that she had no idea what any of them were talking about.

'I didn't tell them what an idiot you felt when you realised that I was the president of the bank and not the layabout you thought I was when you were trying to get an interview.' Gib's eyes gleamed with appreciation as he saw her struggling to come to terms with the sheer nerve of him. 'You were expecting the president to be someone a lot more formidable, weren't you, darling?'

Somehow Phoebe managed to stretch her mouth into a ghastly smile. 'It was quite a surprise,' she said.

'I must say, darling,' said her father, 'you might have told us what Gib did. You just told your mother he worked for a bank, as if he was some teller. I felt a complete fool when I realised!'

'It sounds wonderful, too,' said Lara, equally impressed. 'It's not as if an ethical bank is something to be ashamed of. Not like...I don't know...being an arms dealer or a politician or something.'

Gib put a consoling arm around Phoebe's shoulders. 'But that's exactly what I love about Phoebe. She just doesn't care what I do or how much money I have.' He smiled teasingly into her eyes. 'You love me for what I am, don't you, bunni—' He pretended to catch himself up guiltily. 'Don't you, *honey*?'

'You know exactly how much I love you,' she said, meeting his gaze directly, and he laughed and released her.

'What did you feel when you found out that Gib was actually the president?' Lara asked eagerly. 'You must have felt a bit stupid, didn't you?'

'To tell you the truth,' said Phoebe, a decidedly crisp edge to her voice, 'I didn't believe a word of it!'

'*President*!' she bit out the moment the door to their bedroom closed behind them. The guests had begun to drift away from the reception and they had a couple of hours to recover before they had to go back down for dinner and dancing. 'Couldn't you have chosen something a bit more likely, like Chancellor of the Exchequer or Director General of the United Nations?'

'I always fancied myself running a bank,' said Gib by way of an excuse.

'Why stop at a bank? Why not pretend you were President of the United States?'

'They would have known that wasn't true.'

Phoebe ground her teeth at the reasonableness of his tone. 'Whereas, it's so believable that you should be running your own bank?'

'They did believe me, didn't they?' he replied, unanswerably.

'I thought we agreed that you would stick to our story?' she accused him, wrenching off her hat. She had a massive tension headache, and the champagne she had been reduced to gulping to cope with the stress of Gib's increasingly ridiculous lies hadn't helped any.

'No more variations, we said. Now I'm not only supposed to be engaged to you and spending the night with you, I'm an accessory to illegal impersonation! Have you thought what will happen if J.G. Grieve hears that you've been impersonating him?'

'I don't think that's very likely,' said Gib soothingly. He hadn't been able to resist the temptation to tease Phoebe a little by elaborating on the basic outlines they had agreed. 'How's he going to know what goes on at an obscure English wedding?'

'These people have lawyers, you know,' said Phoebe with a dark look. 'If he sues you, you needn't think I'm going to support you. God, what a day!' she sighed, sinking down onto the edge of the vast four-poster bed and easing off her high-heeled shoes so that she could rub her sore feet.

Flopping back across the bed, she stared tensely up at the embroidered canopy. 'And we've still got tonight to get through!'

CHAPTER SEVEN

'OH, COME on, it hasn't been that bad.' Gib loosened his tie with a sigh of relief as he wandered around the room, inspecting the wood panelling and the magnificent stone fireplace.

'Not for you, maybe,' she grumbled, 'but it's been a nightmare for me, not knowing what ridiculous story you're going to make up next, and just waiting for someone to turn round and spot that you're here under false pretences. I'm going to feel great when that happens, aren't I?'

'Relax,' he said soothingly. 'Everything's fine. You're just tired. What you need is a nice bath.'

Without waiting for her to reply, he disappeared through a door in the panelling, and the next minute Phoebe heard the sound of water gushing into the bath. 'I'll bring you a drink, and you can unwind,' he shouted over the noise. 'You'll feel much better then.'

Phoebe was tempted to tell him that she would be the judge of what would make her feel better, but a wonderful fragrance of foaming bubbles was drifting through into the bedroom and, when it came down to it, the thought of a long hot soak with a long cool drink was immensely appealing. No point in cutting off her nose to spite her face.

So she leant back against the pillows and let Gib run the bath for her. 'Your bath awaits, madam,' he said grandly at last, holding the door open with a flourish.

The bathroom turned out to be almost as impressive as the bedroom. It was panelled throughout, apart from a deep stone window, just wide enough to stick your bow and arrow through. A stuffed bear's head was fixed to the wall. There was a selection of imposing antique chests and, in the middle, a vast claw-footed tub, filled to the brim with scented foam. Averting her eyes from the bear, Phoebe saw that Gib had put fluffy towels conveniently to hand on a wooden chair and set out the tempting array of luxurious freebies provided by the hotel along the side of the bath.

'Thank you,' she muttered, touched in spite of herself by the trouble he had taken.

He smiled at her, that unsettling, daredevil grin that never failed to make her nerves jump alarmingly. 'It's my way of saying I'm sorry,' he said disarmingly. 'I didn't mean to wind you up today.'

'That's OK,' Phoebe said awkwardly, feeling as if the wind had been rather taken out of her sails.

'Now, what would you like to drink?'

'Really, you don't need to—'

'I'll add it to my expenses if that will make you feel better,' Gib offered.

Phoebe wasn't sure whether being reminded that he was only doing his job made her feel better or worse, but decided in the end that the most dignified course of action would be to relent.

'Something long and cold would be wonderful,' she said.

'You get in,' said Gib. 'I'll be back in a minute.'

When he had gone, Phoebe got undressed and stepped into the bath. It was enormous, more of a swimming pool than a bath, and she lay back with a luxurious sigh, immersing herself completely beneath the scented water. Maybe Gib wasn't so bad after all, she thought as she emerged, blowing bubbles out of her mouth, and smoothing the wet hair back from her face.

Perhaps she *had* been overreacting. Gib was right, everyone had accepted him without question and there had been no need for her to be so nervous. She had been wound up about the whole situation, she realised, but in the end it hadn't been the wedding or meeting Ben or fooling her family that had made her nervous. It had been Gib himself, Gib with his glinting, unsettling smile, and his warm hand on her back.

You're beautiful and you're brave, he had told her, and it had been the look in his eyes she had been thinking about when she watched Ben getting married, not the ache in her heart. The look in his eyes and touch of his mouth and the feel of his palm against her cheek.

It would have been much easier if he hadn't kissed her. Really, there had been no need for it, Phoebe scolded herself. If she'd thought, it would have been obvious that no one would expect them to kiss like that in the middle of Ben's wedding. She should have told Gib that it was a stupid idea and pushed him firmly away.

Instead of which she had wrapped her arms around him and pulled him closer and kissed him back. A wave of heat that had nothing whatsoever to do with the bath tingled through her as she remembered how it had felt, and when a sharp knock fell on the door her heart jerked painfully.

'I've got a long, cold G&T here for you,' came Gib's voice. 'If I promise to keep my eyes closed, shall I bring it in to you?'

'Just a minute,' she said on a gasp as she slid decorously beneath the deep layer of bubbles. 'OK,' she called.

Gib handed her the drink with a flourish. It looked wonderful, satisfyingly full of chinking ice cubes, a slice of lime bobbing merrily as the tonic fizzed. Her fingers touched his as she took the glass from him. It was so cold that condensation was trickling down the side, making it hard to hold.

That was the reason Phoebe gave herself for the unsteadiness of her grasp anyway. Nothing whatsoever to do with the warmth of Gib's hand.

'Got it?'

'Yes. Thanks,' she added, and then made another mistake of looking up into his face.

He was studying her with appreciative blue eyes, taking in her bare shoulders rising out of the foam. Her hair was slicked back from her face, unconsciously emphasising her bone structure, and the dark lashes were wet and spiky around the green eyes.

'My pleasure,' he said, smiling.

To her fury, Phoebe felt a blush rising up her throat and seeping into her cheeks. 'I thought you were going to keep your eyes closed?' she said as severely as she could.

'I was afraid I would drop your drink if I did that,' said Gib. 'I'll close them now.'

Shutting them virtuously, he proceeded to make a big show of bumping into things on his way out of the bathroom.

'Idiot!' sighed Phoebe, shaking her head, but in spite of herself she was smiling.

She didn't know whether it was the bath or the gin that did the trick, but she was feeling a million times better when she emerged from the bathroom some time later to find Gib stretched out on the four-poster bed.

He had loosened the shirt at his neck and rolled up his sleeves and was lying with his hands behind his head. He looked lean and lazy, and somehow disturbing, and Phoebe's nerves, which had calmed down while she was in the bath, instantly sprang to the alert again at the sight of him.

Gib turned his head as she came out of the bathroom, wrapped in a towelling robe supplied by the hotel, her skin pink and glowing. There was a tiny pause.

'Better?' he asked after a moment.

'Yes, thank you,' said Phoebe stiffly. She felt ridiculously shy of him again all of a sudden. 'You can have the bathroom now if you want.'

'I'll have a shower in a bit.' He yawned, and suddenly it was as if that moment of tension had never been. 'I'm just enjoying this bed. It's very comfortable. You should try it,' he added, patting the cover beside him and pulling up some pillows invitingly.

Phoebe hesitated. Every instinct told her that climbing into bed next to Gib was asking for trouble, but it was too soon to get changed and the only other place to sit was a wooden chair which was no doubt authentic but which didn't look at all comfortable.

And anyway, she wasn't getting *into* bed with him, she rationalised. She was just getting *onto* it, which was a different matter entirely. Gib just happened to be sitting there as well. What could possibly be awkward about that?

So she clambered up beside him, trying not to expose too much leg beneath the towelling robe. The bed was huge and, as Gib had said, very comfortable. Phoebe leant back against the pillows with a sigh. After the accumulated tensions of the day, it was good to relax for a moment.

'I've always wanted to sleep in a bed like this,' said Gib, breaking the silence that was really quite companionable.

Phoebe, who had been almost asleep, jerked back to attention. It was going to be bad enough getting through the rest of the evening without the prospect of actually getting into bed with Gib to cope with!

'I hope you're not planning on sleeping in one tonight!'

'Where else am I going to sleep?' he asked in a mock injured tone. 'That floor is made of stone!'

Phoebe looked around the room, which was authentically furnished with an austere wooden chair and absolutely no modern innovations like a sofa or even an armchair where she could reasonably expect Gib to make himself comfortable. There were good reasons why they didn't live in the Middle Ages any more.

She sighed inwardly. She supposed the idea of getting married in a castle had seemed very romantic to Ben and Lisa but, when all was said and done, there was nothing wrong with a nice, characterless motel room. Preferably with twin beds.

'You don't think sharing a bed might be a bit intimate given that we're not...that we don't...?' Phoebe trailed off uncomfortably.

'I won't forget you're my boss if that's what you're worried about,' said Gib with one of those lurking smiles of his.

'That's good coming from someone who's spent the entire day forgetting that I'm boss!' she retorted, nettled by his refusal to take the situation seriously.

'Oh, that's a bit of an exaggeration, isn't it?'

'We agreed that you would stick to the story and keep it simple. The second rule of engagement, if you remember? I'm not sure how claiming to be president of an international bank was keeping it simple!'

Gib looked at her and wondered if she had any idea how desirable she looked with her damp, dark hair and her vivid face and her eyes bright and green with irritation.

'I stuck to the important thing, which is that I'm in love with you,' he pointed out. 'You can't get simpler than that. I've kept my side of the bargain, haven't I?' he challenged her.

Phoebe dropped her eyes first. She couldn't deny that he had been very convincing. He was certainly a much better actor than her.

'Yes,' she acknowledged.

'And I said I was sorry,' Gib reminded her, his eyes dancing. 'And I ran you a bath. *And* I bought you a gin and
tonic!'

'On expenses!'

'It's the thought that counts,' he said virtuously. 'I'm trying to do my job as best I can, and if you were a caring
employer, you wouldn't even *consider* making me sleep on
a stone floor! Besides,' he said, patting the expanse of cover
between them, 'this bed could sleep a family of six easily!
And we can always put a pillow down the middle if you
don't think you'll be able to keep your hands off me otherwise,' he added in what Phoebe considered was a spirit
of sheer provocation.

'I don't think *that* will a problem!' she said in a tart voice.

'And I'll keep my hands off you,' he promised, which
somehow didn't make her feel quite as good as it should
have done.

'Please make sure you do!'

'So, can I sleep with you tonight?' asked Gib. 'I know it
won't mean anything and it won't be setting a precedent.
See,' he told her, grinning. 'I haven't forgotten that first rule
of engagement, either!'

'Oh, all right,' said Phoebe, who couldn't be bothered to
argue any longer. 'But I don't want to hear any more stupid
stories this evening,' she warned him, 'or you'll be sleeping
on the floor after all. I don't care how cold it is!'

They only had a couple of hours before they had to return
for dinner and dancing but, to Phoebe, lying next to Gib on
that big bed, it was quite long enough. It wasn't that he was
restless or said anything she could object to, and the bed
was so wide that there was no danger of brushing against
him accidentally.

It was just that whenever she closed her eyes all she could
see was his smile dancing behind her eyelids, and the mo-

ment she snapped them open, they would stray sideways to where he lay beside her, managing to fill all the available space with the sheer force of his personality even when he was at his most lazy and relaxed.

All in all, it was a relief when Gib went off to have a shower. Phoebe took the opportunity to scramble off the bed and change into the dress she had brought specially for that evening. It was very simple, a slim sheath the colour of a tropical lagoon that brought out the green in her eyes and left her shoulders bare. Phoebe had worried that it might be a little too dramatic for her to carry off, but Kate and Bella had been unanimous in their approval.

'It's perfect! No one would ever think you were broken-hearted in a dress like that!'

'That,' Kate had agreed, 'is a dress worn by a woman in control of her life.'

There was irony for you, thought Phoebe, wondering what to do with her hair. She *never* felt in control when Gib was around.

The bathroom door opened and Gib came out, a towel wrapped around his hips. He whistled when he saw her, and she span round, the breath drying in her throat. His blonde hair was dark and damp from the shower, and she couldn't help noticing how lean and brown and compactly muscled his body was. Quickly, she turned back to the mirror where she was fixing slides into her hair.

'I hope you're not planning to go like that,' she said, horrified by the shake in her voice.

'I wish I could.' Gib contemplated his suit without enthusiasm. 'I suppose I'll have to put that on again. I've got nothing else to wear, and before you say it, yes, I know it's my fault! I hate wearing suits,' he grumbled as he retrieved his shirt from the hanger. 'I can't stand the feel of a tie around my neck.'

'I'm surprised you're not used to it, running that bank of yours,' said Phoebe, taking refuge in sarcasm to distract herself from view of his smooth brown back in the mirror.

He glanced at her over his shoulder with a glimmering smile. 'Maybe mine's a different kind of bank where you don't have to dress like a dummy all day!'

'That sounds about as likely as you being president,' she said, mumbling through the clips she was holding in her mouth while she secured her hair in place. 'Don't you want your staff to look professional?'

'In my bank we're more concerned with what people do than how they look,' Gib informed her loftily.

Phoebe smoothed the last hair into place. 'Right,' she said, her voice laced with irony. 'I'm sure it's a great success! Now look, can you please keep off the subject of banks this evening? We don't want to be rumbled now we've got this far. I'd appreciate it if you'd remember what you're here to do!'

'To show everyone how in love with you I am?'

'Yes,' she said, not quite able to meet his eyes directly. She busied herself looking for the necklace Bella had insisted on lending her instead.

'That shouldn't be a problem with the way you look tonight,' said Gib. 'You look sensational!'

Startled, Phoebe's eyes flew involuntarily to meet his in the mirror. He was smiling, obviously joking, but there had been something in his voice that made her suddenly, acutely, aware of him, of the breadth of his shoulders and the long, muscled legs and the easy way he moved.

'There's no need to start pretending yet,' she said, tearing her gaze away with an uncertain laugh. 'There's nobody else here.'

'I know,' said Gib.

The air leaked out of Phoebe's lungs, and in the taut

silence that followed, she fumbled around on the chest of drawers for her jewellery. She was intensely relieved when Gib went back into the bathroom. He reappeared wearing trousers, which was something, she thought. Shrugging on his shirt, he looped the tie round his neck and knotted it loosely.

The casual intimacy of dressing threw Phoebe completely. She was trying to fasten Bella's spectacular necklace, and Gib's presence only made her fingers even clumsier at the fiddly catch, until she muttered under her breath in frustration.

'Here, let me have a go,' he offered, having watched her struggling for a few moments.

It would be childish to refuse, Phoebe decided. She bent her head, tensing as Gib moved towards her and brushed her hair gently out of the way. The graze of his fingers against her neck made her shiver involuntarily, and she stood mouse-still as he fastened the necklace and smoothed it into place.

There it was done. But instead of stepping back with the flip comment she half expected, Gib let his hands rest for a moment on the curve of her shoulders. Slowly, almost unwillingly, Phoebe lifted her head and met his eyes, blue and serious, in the mirror. They had held the same expression after he had kissed her in the car and her heart began to slam in her chest. She couldn't move, could just stand there feeling the warmth of his hands on her skin, while an answering heat uncoiled inside her at an alarming rate.

With an enormous effort, she moistened her lips. 'We'd better finish getting ready,' she managed, appalled at the huskiness of her voice. Clearing her throat, she tried again. 'We'll be late.'

Gib dropped his hands and stepped back. 'We don't want that,' he agreed dryly. 'They might think that two people as much in love as we are have got better things to do alone here with a four-poster bed than get dressed up in uncomfortable clothes to spend an evening making more small talk!'

'Making small talk was part of the deal,' she reminded him, still not quite as steadily as she would have liked.

'Ah, yes, the deal, we mustn't forget that!'

They walked across the courtyard from their tower in silence. Phoebe was desperately aware of Gib, close beside her but not touching. There was a strange, jittery feeling just below her skin, and her stomach was looping and churning in a way that made her wish she could go back to simply worrying about whether anyone would spot that Gib wasn't really a banker and wasn't really her lover. That had seemed bad enough at the time, but this new consciousness of Gib was much, much worse, this was a whole new level of nervousness and Phoebe didn't like it at all.

For dinner the remaining guests were divided up among five round tables. Phoebe and Gib were sitting with Lara, who spent most of her time moaning about her parents and their unreasonable behaviour in disapproving of her latest boyfriend.

'He's got his own band,' Lara confided. 'Some guy in the music business came to listen to one of their gigs, and he thinks they've got a great future. They're going to London soon to make a recording, not that that cuts any ice with Mum and Dad! They're so conventional,' she grumbled. 'They can't bear the fact that Jed lives in a squat. They don't understand that he's an artist. He'd be stifled in an ordinary environment. That's why he didn't get an invitation to come to the wedding, even though we've been going out for *weeks* now! They want me to find someone like Gib, with a proper job.'

Involuntarily, Phoebe glanced at Gib. 'Nice to know that

someone appreciates how hard I work,' he murmured provocatively.

'Oh, they think you're great,' said Lara, missing the
irony. 'Mum can't wait for you to spend the weekend so
she can interrogate you properly! You'd better brace yourself, Phoebe. She's bound to get out the baby photographs
and tell Gib about the time you took your knickers off in
the middle of their sherry party.'

'I was only three,' said Phoebe as Gib raised an enquiring
eyebrow.

'At least Jed is spared that,' said Lara, cheering up at the
realisation. 'You should have been a rebel, Gib, then they
wouldn't be so keen on inviting you to stay.'

Oh, dear, Phoebe sighed inwardly. She should have fore-
seen that her mother would start planning intimate family
get-togethers. Now she would have to think up endless excuses as to why they couldn't go down for the weekend
until their supposedly perfect relationship had had time to
fall apart convincingly.

But how could she think when Gib was sitting next to
her, and she was aware of every time he lifted his glass or
gestured, every time he turned his head towards her and his
smile burned at the edge of her vision. Her shoulders were
still tingling where his hands had rested. The image of how
he had looked when he came out of the bathroom with his
powerful shoulders and his bare, brown chest and his
straight, strong legs shimmered in front of Phoebe's eyes no
matter how hard she tried to blink it away so that she could
see the medallions of lamb on her plate.

Not that she could eat, anyway. She pushed the food dis-
tractedly around her plate and tried to decide whether she
longed for the evening to end, or dreaded, because it would
mean being alone with Gib again.

And that bed.

Phoebe gulped at her wine. She must stop thinking about Gib like this! Stop thinking about his mouth and his hands and his lean, hard body. If Kate and Bella were here, she was sure they would tell her that she was simply projecting her feelings for Ben onto Gib because he was handy.

Yes, that was all it was. She was trying to turn him into some substitute for Ben. Ridiculous, really. So all she had to do was concentrate on Ben and maybe her pounding pulse would calm down and the twitchy feeling would fade and the tight knot in her stomach would relax.

It was hard to think about Ben when she couldn't see him, but once the pudding had been removed, the music struck up and bride and groom took to the little dance floor to much sentimental sighing from the other guests. This gave Phoebe the opportunity she needed, and she turned her chair like many of the other guests so that she could watch Ben holding Lisa close. He looked very contented, she thought. Not the most exciting man in the world, perhaps, but contented.

Where had *that* thought come from? Phoebe caught herself up with a frown. She had never found Ben at all dull before, so there was no reason to start thinking it now, just because he was so different from Gib, Gib with his gleaming blue eyes and his unsettling smile and his ability to make her furious and want to laugh at the same time.

Turning her back deliberately on him, she made herself focus on Ben, and after a while, as people were starting to move around, Gib got up and went over to talk to her parents. Phoebe was still staring determinedly at the dance floor, but she might as well have been looking straight at him, so acutely was she aware of every move he made. She was watching Ben, but all her senses were attuned to Gib as he sat down next to her parents. She didn't need to see him to know that his alert, mobile face was lit with laughter, or that his hands were gesticulating as he talked.

'Phoebe!'

She started as her mother came to take Gib's empty chair. 'Phoebe,' she demanded in an urgent undertone, 'what on earth do you think you are doing?'

From the other side of the room, Gib saw Phoebe stiffen and her chin came up at a combative angle. He didn't know what her mother was saying to her, but it obviously wasn't going down at all well. Phoebe's face was flushed and there was a dangerous glitter to her eyes.

Murmuring an excuse, he got to his feet and went over. 'Come on, Phoebe,' he said as he held out his hand. 'Let's dance.'

Phoebe went without a word. She let him pull her into his arms and was glad of the excuse to hide her face in his throat. She felt ridiculously shaky all of a sudden. Gib held her tightly in a way that was at once comforting and disturbing. She was very aware of the hardness of his body, of the masculine scent of his skin, of the warmth of his hands through the silky material of her dress.

Gib could feel her trembling, and his expression was wry. Seeing Ben dancing with his new bride must have been the final straw for her today, and whatever her mother had been saying to her obviously hadn't helped. Pulling her onto the dance floor had been an instinctive act to offer her an escape, but he hadn't counted on how hard it would be for him. She was so warm and so slender, and her dress slipped distractingly over her skin beneath his hands. He could smell her perfume and feel her soft breath and the tickle of her eyelashes against his throat, the silky hair beneath his cheek.

A friend, he reminded himself. That was all he was supposed to be. A friend was what Phoebe needed right now, and he should be thinking about how much she was hurting rather than about how much he would like to take her back to that four-poster bed and make her forget all about Ben, and make her smile again.

In the meantime, she needed him to carry on the pretence, Gib told himself. If nothing else, it was a pretext to pull her closer, to kiss her ear and smooth his hand down her spine, feeling the dress shift tantalisingly over her bare skin.

It was just part of the act, after all. If he was really her lover, he wouldn't want to let her go when the music stopped, would he? He wouldn't want to take her back to the table and share her with everybody else. He would take her out into the summer night where he could kiss her properly in the darkness.

Almost without thinking, he found himself steering Phoebe out through the open French windows and onto the terrace. She didn't resist, but when they came to a halt at last in the shadows, she pulled back to look at him, her eyes huge and dark in her pale face.

'Thank you for that,' she said with a crooked smile. 'Mum and I were about to come to blows!'

Gib made himself let her go. 'What was she saying to you?'

'Oh, she came over to tick me off for ignoring you.' The shadows hid the flush that crept up Phoebe's cheeks as she remembered what her mother had said. She had been furious with Phoebe for sitting and mooning openly over Ben, as she thought.

'You told us that you were over Ben,' she had accused her. 'You said that you were in love with Gib. It certainly doesn't look that way from where we're sitting,' she had swept on when Phoebe had tried to protest. 'It looks as if you've just been using Gib as a way to get back at Ben somehow. That's not fair, Phoebe. It's not fair to Ben and it's not fair to Gib.'

There had been a lot more along the same lines. Trapped, Phoebe had been unable to explain that watching Ben had only been a way of not watching Gib.

'Mum thought we'd had a row,' she told him. 'She's afraid I'm going to lose you by being too uncompromising.'

'Shall I tell her I like you that way?' said Gib.

Her smile glimmered in the dusky light. 'I'm not sure she would believe you. In Mum's world, women are sweet and subservient and agree with everything their husbands say.'

'Sounds like a parallel universe to me,' he commented dryly.

'Exactly. Anyway,' Phoebe went on awkwardly after a minute, 'I owe you an apology.'

'Oh?'

'After everything I had to say about you sticking to the script, I'm the one that's made Mum suspicious,' she said with difficulty. 'She thinks I'm just using you and that I'm still in love with Ben.'

Sheila Lane was no fool, Gib thought, and she must know her daughter better than anyone. If she thought Phoebe was still in love with Ben, it was probably true.

'We'd better convince her that's not true, then, hadn't we?' he said, deliberately brisk. 'What do you want to do? Another smoochy dance?'

Phoebe looked at him then away. This was her chance. 'No,' she said, and then had to stop and take a breath. 'I want you to kiss me.'

It came out more abruptly than she had intended. 'If you don't mind,' she added hastily.

Gib looked at her with rather a twisted smile. 'Sure, if that's what you want,' he said.

He didn't sound exactly thrilled at the prospect, Phoebe

noted with a sinking heart. It had seemed reasonable enough when she had first thought of it, sensible even. What was the point of obsessing about that kiss this morning, when she could just get the whole thing out of her system by kissing him again? she had reasoned. It wouldn't be the same this time, and it might at least keep her mother quiet. It wasn't that she *wanted* him to kiss her particularly. It was just part of the act.

'I don't want to force you,' she said defensively. 'Of course you don't have to if you don't want to.'

He shrugged. 'It's no big deal. I'm getting paid, remember?' he pointed out. 'You might as well get your money's worth.'

Well, there was one way of taking any romance out of the situation.

Phoebe wished she had never started this, but it was too late to back out now.

And, as Gib had so coolly reminded her, she was paying him good money for this. Why shouldn't she ask him to kiss her? The fact that she had been thinking about it all evening was neither here nor there.

'Shall we move back where your mother can see us more clearly?' Gib was saying briskly.

Without waiting for an answer, he took her by the waist and manoeuvred her as if she were a rather unwieldy piece of furniture until they were on the edge of the light spilling out from the French windows, where they would be visible while looking as if they had meant to conceal themselves in the shadows.

In spite of his deliberately prosaic attitude, Phoebe's senses jolted with anticipation as Gib's hands tightened against her. Her heart was thudding in slow, painful strokes, and the excitement building inside her was so intense that she abruptly lost her nerve.

'M-maybe this isn't such a good idea after all,' she croaked, but she didn't move and her hands seemed to be creeping up his arms as if they had a will of their own.

'Oh, I think it is,' said Gib in an odd voice. He pulled her close, and when his mouth came down on hers Phoebe's momentary hesitation evaporated in a rush of sensation.

His lips were warm and sure and persuasive as they explored hers. He might not have been too keen on the idea initially, but it certainly didn't seem to be too much of a hardship for him now. That might be a sign of a man expert in dealing with women, but Phoebe was beyond caring one way or another. She gave herself up to the sheer pleasure of being held hard against him and, as his hands drifted enticingly down her back, she wrapped her arms around his neck and kissed him back.

God, it felt wonderful! It was all Phoebe could do to hang on to the last vestiges of her self-control but somewhere she found the will-power to unhook her arms from round his neck. Reluctantly, she broke the kiss, and took a ragged breath.

'I think that should do the trick,' she said.

CHAPTER EIGHT

FOR a split second, Gib looked blank, and then his hands dropped. 'Right,' he said tonelessly.

The momentary blaze of expression in his eyes gave Phoebe pause but, just as she was about to apologise, she saw him smile again, and the words dried on her tongue. He was a little too expert at this kissing business, she told herself. A little too cool in the way he took her in his arms, as if she was just the latest in a very long line of women who had begged him to kiss them.

'Thanks,' she said instead, steadying her voice with an effort. 'That was fine.'

Gib's smile faded. Fine? he thought savagely. She had melted into his kiss and kissed him back as if he was the only man in the world she wanted. She knew damn well it had been more than fine for both of them!

He couldn't believe that she had really just been acting to convince her mother that they hadn't had a row. Still, if that was the way she wanted to play it, it was up to her. He shrugged.

'It's all part of the service,' he told her.

The coolness in his voice rather daunted Phoebe. He might at least pretend that it had been more than a rather tiresome part of his job!

Now he actually had the nerve to glance at his watch. 'Do you think we've spent long enough out here, or do you want to kiss again?' he asked in a bored tone.

Phoebe couldn't help flinching. He obviously couldn't wait to get inside. Probably terrified she was going to insist on being kissed again. Oh, God, what if he thought it was all an elaborate ruse to get her hands on him? After the way she had kissed him back, he must think that she was absolutely desperate and was probably even now making up excuses in case she threw herself at him in the night!

Mortified, she retreated behind an air of prickly hauteur. 'No, I think that was quite enough,' she said.

Back in the banqueting hall, it was obvious that her mother had seen the kiss and was looking satisfied. She didn't even raise her eyebrows when Phoebe went to talk to friends on another table, leaving Gib with Lara.

On her mettle, Phoebe was on sparkling form. She was determined to show Gib that she was quite as unaffected by that kiss out on the terrace as he was. That meant keeping an eye on whether he was noticing or not but, infuriatingly, he hardly seemed to be aware of her at all.

He had loosened his tie and was relaxed in his chair, chatting easily to the others on the table. If nothing else, his part required him to look as if he cared where she was and what she was doing, thought Phoebe piqued, and when she saw him take to the floor with Lara, her eyes narrowed dangerously. They didn't need to look as if they were having quite such a good time!

She was so busy trying not to watch Gib dancing with her sister that she hardly noticed when Ben joined the table where she was sitting. He and Lisa were obviously circulating. Phoebe listened with half an ear, laughing at all the right points, but her mind was on Gib, and Ben had to ask her to dance twice before he could gain her attention.

'For old-time's sake,' he said.

Over his shoulder, Phoebe could see Gib laughing with Lara as they went back to their table, and she smiled brilliantly at Ben as she got to her feet. 'That would be lovely!'

It was odd to be dancing with Ben again. Phoebe felt

awkward and unfamiliar in his arms, as if he were a stranger rather than the man she had once planned to spend her entire life with, and she couldn't help comparing it with the way she had felt when she was dancing with Gib. The thought wiped the glittering smile from her face and made her stumble.

The next instant Gib was beside them. 'I think it's my turn now,' he said. He was smiling, but something in his face made Ben release Phoebe with alacrity.

'What do you think you're doing?' she demanded as Ben made good his escape and Gib calmly pulled her into his arms to continue the dance.

'My job,' he said. 'You're paying me to act like a besotted lover, and believe me, no lover could sit and watch you looking at your ex-fiancé like that.'

'We were just having a dance for old-time's sake,' Phoebe protested. 'There was no need for you to barge in and embarrass me!'

'Oh, you think that was embarrassing, did you? You want to try making jolly conversation with the other wedding guests while your supposed fiancée makes it blatantly obvious that she's still in love with the bridegroom! What was the point of us going through this whole pretence if you're going to dance with Ben like that?' he demanded furiously.

Phoebe opened her mouth and then shut it again as it hit her for the first time that she wasn't in love with Ben any longer. She had got so used to him being part of her life, that she hadn't even realised that he wasn't there any more.

But she couldn't tell Gib that. She had made such a fuss about Ben and how desperate she was to save face that she couldn't admit now that none of it had been necessary. He would think that it had just been an excuse to spend time with him, and Phoebe wasn't having him wondering why she had responded so eagerly to the kiss that she had ordered if *that* was the case.

She didn't even want to wonder about it herself.

No, much better for Gib to think that she was still in love with Ben.

'I can't help how I feel,' she said.

'He's married,' said Gib brutally, 'and you're supposed to be in love with me.'

'Just for tonight!' Phoebe reminded him.

She felt oddly detached. Here they were, both wearing fixed smiles and arguing through clenched teeth as they moved mechanically in time to the music, and all the time a part of her couldn't help noticing how good it felt to have his arms around her, how oddly familiar his body felt after Ben's.

If Gib was conscious of a similar sense of recognition, he gave absolutely no sign of it. For once the lazy good-humour was entirely absent. His jaw was taut and a tell-tale muscle twitched tensely in his cheek.

'Yes, I know,' he gritted. 'I'm only being paid for twenty-four hours! Any longer and I'll start asking for a bonus.'

'Don't count on it—twenty-four hours will be more than enough!'

They glared at each other for a moment before Gib pulled her roughly against him. 'Might as well make it look as if we can't keep our hands off each other,' he said, laying his cheek against her hair. Phoebe held herself rigid at first but, realising how ridiculous she must look, she succumbed to temptation eventually and let herself relax against him.

Just for show, of course.

Only it wasn't that easy. His closeness was having a strange effect on her insides, which felt as if they were un-looping and unravelling with an alarming momentum while her heart had set up a slow, irregular thudding that drowned out the music and the laughter around them and left nothing but the smell of Gib's skin, and the faint roughness of his jaw and the solid strength of his body where he held her against him.

'What was he saying to you anyway?' Gib asked as if the words had been forced out of him.

'Who?' said Phoebe, momentarily disorientated by his abrupt question.

'Ben,' he said impatiently. 'I saw him whispering sweet nothings in your ear. You'd never guess that he'd only been married a few hours!'

'If you must know, he was telling me that he thought you and I were made for each other, and that he was glad that I was so happy. Ironic, don't you think?'

Gib snorted dismissively. 'He's only saying that because it suits him to believe it. If he knew you at all, he wouldn't think you were happy. Even I can see you're miserable.'

'Well, that's where you're wrong,' said Phoebe, putting up her chin. 'All I wanted was for this to be a happy day for everyone, especially Ben, and it has been. That's enough to make me happy.

'I should thank you,' she went on as she spotted an opportunity to convince Gib that she had just been using him and that when she had responded to his kisses, it had been strictly according to their first rule of engagement. 'I don't think I would have been able to convince everyone on my own, but I have to say you played your part to perfection. You should take up acting if your business plans don't take off.'

'There's no need to thank me,' he said shortly. 'You're paying me.'

'Still, I appreciate it,' she persevered, rather proud of her casual tone. 'There were a lot of little touches that really made a difference, like that kiss out on the terrace.'

A 'little touch'? Was that all it had been to her? Gib's jaw clenched. *He* was the one who was always first to back out of a relationship the moment it threatened to get too emotional. It was a new experience to be given the brush-off at this stage, and Gib didn't like it much.

Had his attitude rankled with all those women he'd dated the way Phoebe's coolness was grating on him? he found himself wondering with a trace of compunction. Not getting involved was the sensible option, but when you were on the receiving end, it wasn't a nice feeling.

'It's OK,' he said in a curt voice. 'I'm not expecting a tip! Anyway, it wasn't difficult.'

Right, what was a heart-shaking kiss here and there to a man like Gib? thought Phoebe with a touch of resentment.

'Good,' she said a little stiffly.

'It's easier when you're not emotionally involved,' Gib went on with a shrug.

Yes, all right, she had got that point. Phoebe pressed her lips together in a thin line.

'I'm glad it's been such easy money for you,' she said, unable to keep an acid edge from her voice.

Gib thought about kissing her, about the way she felt in his arms now, about the night to come when he was going to have to lie next to her in that damned four-poster bed and not touch her.

'I wouldn't put it quite like that,' he said.

Using Gib's flight to Switzerland as an excuse, they left early the next morning before anyone else was up.

Getting up early wasn't a problem, at least not for Phoebe. She had hardly slept the night before. The evening had seemed interminable. Part of her had longed for it to be over so that she could escape, while another part dreaded being alone with Gib.

When they got back to the room, the bed had been turned down invitingly in the light of a bedside lamp, the perfect setting for romance. Gib closed the heavy door with a clunk of the old-fashioned iron key, and silence settled like a blanket around them, stifling all the oxygen from the air and making it hard to breathe.

Phoebe's heart was battering in her throat and her breath was coming in short, jerky gasps. She was appalled by her spiralling thoughts. This was absolutely not the time to start obsessing about Gib's mouth and Gib's hands, not the time to think about his body or what it would be like if they were the lovers they had pretended to be all day, but she couldn't help it.

Gib had continued to play his part in front of the others, but as soon as they were alone he had become cool and distant. Phoebe was confused by how much she missed the gleaming mockery in eyes and the slow smile that had so unsettled her before. It seemed like a lifetime since she had found him irritating.

Now she stood just inside the door, her eyes skittering frantically around the room in an effort not to look at him. There was a quivering deep inside her, a certain knowledge that if he turned to her now and smiled she wouldn't be able to resist him, so when he did turn, she caught her breath.

He even smiled, but it was a perfunctory smile at best and he was thinking not of romance but of the practical arrangements about how they would sleep. She didn't need to worry, he told her. They would put a pillow down the middle of the bed in time-honoured fashion and she could sleep easy. 'I haven't forgotten those rules of yours,' he said, and Phoebe reminded herself that she had better not forget them either.

The bed was huge and there was plenty of room for both of them, but that didn't stop Phoebe being agonisingly aware of Gib all night. Not that her closeness seemed to bother *him*, she realised resentfully. He simply stretched out and went to sleep without any problem, leaving her to toss and turn restlessly all night.

By the time morning came, Phoebe was gritty-eyed, but she had given herself a good talking to during those long, sleepless hours, and she was determined to get back to normal. From now on she would be as brisk and businesslike as Gib had been.

'Perhaps this is an appropriate time to pay you,' she said when Gib emerged from the bathroom, dressed once again in his suit. 'Is a cheque all right?' she added, picking up her handbag. 'Or would you prefer cash?'

The muscle in Gib's jaw tightened momentarily. 'A cheque's fine.'

'Good.' Phoebe made big deal of finding her cheque-book and then a pen. 'Now, who should I make it out to?'

'J. Gibson,' said Gib, after only the tiniest of hesitations.

Scribbling her signature, Phoebe handed the cheque to him. He gave it a cursory glance, and then frowned. 'This is more than we agreed.'

'Well, it all went according to plan,' she said carelessly. 'I thought you deserved a bonus.' There, if that didn't show him that she had been treating the whole weekend as a purely business arrangement, nothing would!

Gib looked at her for a moment, then tucked the cheque into the pocket of his shirt. 'Thanks,' he said in a voice empty of all expression.

It was a largely silent drive back to London, with conversation limited to stilted comments about the traffic. Unable to think of a good reason why she should be tense or nervous, Phoebe said that she would drive, but perversely she felt both. It was something to do with the fact that Gib was sitting beside her, not frowning, not sulking, just looking neutral. Phoebe was horrified at how much she missed his smile. She couldn't help comparing this trip with the drive down, only the day before, when they had laughed as they invented explanations for the ending of their supposed romance.

Now it seemed all too obvious that even an invented romance between them was doomed to disaster. No one seeing them together this morning would have any trouble in believing that it would all end in tears.

A sigh escaped Phoebe as she waited to turn onto the main road and, hearing it, she pulled herself up sharply. There was no reason for her to feel this depressed. She had got through Ben's wedding better than she could have hoped, Gib had played his part, she had paid him as agreed, and that was the end of the matter. The sooner she got back to London and normality, the better.

Phoebe had hoped that their early start would mean that they could sneak into the house while Kate and Bella were still asleep, thereby avoiding instant interrogation, but a traffic jam near Heathrow meant that by the time they got back, the other two girls were drinking coffee at the kitchen table, yawning and bleary-eyed but definitely awake.

Gib disappeared, muttering about changing out of his suit at last, so Phoebe was left alone to undergo a detailed cross-examination about the wedding. The girls began easily enough, insisting that she describe key outfits, especially the bride's dress, and wanting to know whether there had been any hats to rival Phoebe's, but any hope she might have had that they might leave it at that was soon quashed. Kate told her severely that they were just warming up. She was to tell them about Ben, about how he had been with her and how she had felt, and how Lisa had treated her, but all the time Phoebe could feel them building up to the key question.

It was Bella who voiced it in the end. 'So,' she asked in an oh-so-casual kind of way, 'how did you and Gib get on?'

'Fine,' said Phoebe brightly.

'He ended up spending the night then?'

'Mmmnn,' she said, getting up to pour herself some more coffee.

'Did you have to share a room?'

'What?' Phoebe busied herself finding some milk in the fridge. 'Oh…yes, yes we did.'

'And?'

'And nothing,' she said. 'What did you expect? A night of wild passion?' She even managed a laugh, as if she hadn't spent half the night wondering *exactly* what that would be like. 'You don't really think I would have felt like that, having just seen the love of my life get married, do you?' she went on, making sure that they got the point. 'Honestly, it was just a perfectly straightforward arrangement for both of us, and before you ask, yes, we *did* kiss a couple of times, and it didn't mean anything at all. It was just part of the act.'

'That's right,' Gib's voice came from behind her, and Phoebe span round, slopping coffee.

He had changed into jeans and a T-shirt, so he looked more like the Gib she remembered, but she noticed that his smile had the faint edge it had worn since the night before, and her heart, which had lurched at the sound of his voice, sank inexplicably.

Gib came over to the table and dropped a careless hand on Phoebe's shoulder. 'Yes, it was all just an act, wasn't it, Phoebe? The easiest money I've ever earned,' he added to Kate and Bella, while Phoebe was burningly conscious of the warmth of his hand through her shirt. 'I've even got the cheque to prove it,' he said.

*   *   *

It was all just an act. They had been her own words, but over the next couple of weeks, Phoebe found herself resenting them more and more. If it was all just an act, why couldn't she forget about those kisses, the way Gib so obviously had? She kept thinking about how he had taken her cheque and put it in his pocket. Easy money, he had called it.

Phoebe couldn't understand what was wrong with her. She was usually so good at being sensible. She was famous for her ability to pull herself together and get on with things. Even at her lowest point, when Ben had told her that he didn't love her any more, she had clamped down on the hurt and listened while everyone told her how well she was dealing with it. She was doing just the right thing in putting on a brave face, they said, but it had seemed to Phoebe that she didn't have any choice in the matter. She had to just carry on. It was that or fall apart altogether.

So if she had been able to get on with her life then, why couldn't she do it now? There was no point in endlessly reliving the feel of his lips and the touch of his hands and the taste of his mouth. No point in thinking about how good it had felt to be held against him. And certainly no point in wishing that he hadn't overheard her telling Kate and Bella that his kisses had meant nothing to her and that Ben was still the love of her life.

Gib wasn't wasting his time remembering that weekend. He had reverted to his old self, and was as laid-back and lazily cheerful as ever. Once or twice, Phoebe felt his blue eyes on her, but when she glanced at him she saw only the familiar, mocking gleam. He was charming, friendly and funny, and he treated her exactly like Kate and Bella.

Phoebe knew that she should have been relieved. That weekend at Ben's wedding might never have happened for all Gib referred to it. Anyone would think, she thought sometimes, that he had never kissed her at all. Which was just what she wanted.

Only it didn't stop her feeling vaguely disgruntled about it all the same.

Restless and on edge, Phoebe threw herself into her job. To her relief, the programme about the Community Bank had been put on the back-burner while they worked frantically to finish another film, and she spent long days in the edit suite, watching it being cut together before rushing back to the office to sort out the fact that all the sound turned out to be distorted and to arrange for extra footage for one of the key interviews.

Tired as she was at the end of the day, the moment she walked back in the door and saw Gib, he was all she could think about. Matters were not helped by her mother who kept ringing up to tell her how much everyone had liked Gib, and to ask when she was going to bring him down for the weekend.

'I do wish you would, Phoebe,' she pleaded. 'We'd so like to see him again, and maybe you could talk to Lara when you're here,' she added with a sigh. 'She's being so *difficult* about this ghastly boy she's seeing at the moment. He's got rings through every available part of his anatomy, as far as I can see, and his hair is so *dirty*! It makes your father feel ill just to look at him. Why can't she find someone like Gib?'

Phoebe prevaricated as best as she could. Her mother was obviously so worked up about Lara, that she couldn't bring herself to tell her that her supposed engagement was off and that Gib had turned out to be not so wonderful after all. Also, that would have meant discussing the whole matter with Gib, and somehow Phoebe hadn't been able to bring herself to do that.

'I've told Mum there's a crisis at your bank and that

you're very busy,' she told him stiltedly, just in case her mother got him on the phone next time. 'You haven't forgotten that you're president of your very own bank, have you?' she asked with a hint of her old spice.

'Ah, yes, so I am.' Gib tipped back in his chair with his arms behind his head, and his eyes glinted. 'I must find out how they're managing without me!'

'I can see that you've been in a real fret about it!'

'No point in fretting,' he said. 'I trust my staff. There's no point in paying them good salaries if I have to do all the working and worrying myself.'

'I can't imagine you doing either of those things,' said Phoebe. 'Don't you ever get bored lazing around all day?'

Gib let his chair legs drop back to the floor. 'What makes you think I do that?'

'Observation!'

'You haven't been watching me closely enough, Phoebe,' he said with one of his gleaming smiles. 'It just so happens that I work while you're out.'

'Doing what?' she asked suspiciously.

'I've been setting up a project,' he told her. 'It's all looking pretty good, as a matter of fact. I'm hoping to finalise everything before too long, and then I'll be out of your hair.'

Phoebe felt as if she had walked into a wall in the dark. 'You're leaving?'

'I have to leave some time,' said Gib.

'Oh.' Phoebe tried to swallow the desolate feeling in her throat. It was almost as if she wanted to cry, which was ridiculous. 'When?' she asked, and then, afraid that it sounded too abrupt, 'I mean, I'll have to find another lodger.'

'I'm not sure yet,' he said. 'I'll let you know.'

'Fine.' She looked down at her hands. 'We'll miss you,'

she said, and it was as if the words came out of their own accord.

'Will you?'

'Of course,' she said brightly, suddenly nervous. 'We've got used to having you here.'

'No, will *you* miss me?'

Something in his voice compelled her to meet the intense blue gaze, and when she did it was as if the air was evaporating around her, shortening her breath and making her heart batter against her ribs. She wanted to laugh and give him a flip answer, the way he would have done in the same situation, but somehow she couldn't.

'Yes,' she admitted. 'Yes, I will.'

Gib's chair scraped over the tiles as he got to his feet. 'Phoebe,' he began urgently, only to break off as the doorbell pealed imperatively.

'I'll get it,' Bella's voice shouted as she clattered down the stairs. 'It'll be Josh.'

Gib hesitated. Bella was never ready to go out, which meant that Josh would come into the kitchen and have a drink while he waited, the way he always did.

Phoebe was waiting expectantly, but he couldn't talk to her now. 'It doesn't matter,' he said flatly, and turned towards the fridge instead. 'I'll get Josh a beer.'

But it wasn't Josh. It was Lara, carrying a bulging bag and wearing a defiant expression.

Bella showed her into the kitchen, grimacing warningly at Phoebe from behind Lara's shoulder.

'Lara!' Phoebe hurried over to hug her sister. 'What on earth are you doing here?'

'I've come to stay.'

'What?' She did a double take as she stepped back from the hug.

'Jed's come up to London with his band,' said Lara.

'They've got some gigs lined up, and they're going to make a recording. This could be their big break. Mum and Dad are delighted, of course,' she added bitterly. 'They're hoping that I'll forget all about him now that he's left, but I won't, I *won't!*'

Her voice rose alarmingly. She looked exhausted, thought Phoebe in concern, making her sit down in the armchair.

'Of course, you won't,' she said soothingly. 'I know Jed's important to you…but wouldn't you rather stay with him in that case?'

Lara sniffed dolefully. 'He doesn't know I'm coming,' she was forced to admit. 'He thinks I'm too spoilt and that I wouldn't be able to live rough the way he does, but I wouldn't mind if only I could be with him.'

Her blue eyes swam with tears as she looked at her sister. 'He didn't believe me when I said I'd give up my course and follow him to London, but if I turn up at the gig tomorrow night, he'll have to take me seriously, won't he?'

Remembering what her parents had told her about Jed, Phoebe wasn't so sure. Pierced he might be, but it sounded like Jed had her little sister sussed. Lara was just as spoilt as he had said, and Phoebe didn't think she would enjoy living in a squat at all, whatever she said now.

'I won't stay long,' Lara was saying earnestly. 'Just until I can convince Jed that I really want to be with him.'

'The thing is, there's not that much room with Gib living here now,' Phoebe prevaricated, hoping that Lara wouldn't remember the layout of the house, and be instantly disappointed.

'You must still have that little spare room that Caro had before she married,' she pointed out immediately.

'Yes, but—' Phoebe stopped. She had been about to say that Gib was sleeping there, but of course Lara would assume that she and Gib would be sharing a room since she still hadn't broken off their mythical engagement. They could always tell Lara the truth, of course, but it was all too complicated to go into at the moment.

'I won't be any trouble,' Lara was pleading. 'It'll only be for a few days and then I'm sure I'll be able to move in with Jed. 'Oh, *please*, Phoebe!' she wailed as Phoebe still hesitated. 'You don't know what it means to me!'

Harassed, Phoebe found herself looking helplessly at Gib. Lara might think that Jed was all she wanted to make her happy, but Phoebe wasn't so sure, and she knew that she shouldn't encourage Lara to abandon yet another course. But, short of turning her little sister out onto the street, she didn't see what else she could do.

'What do you think?' she appealed to Gib. If they really were engaged, she would ask his opinion, wouldn't she?

'I think it's too late for Lara to go anywhere else tonight, so she might as well make herself comfortable and we'll sort something out in the morning,' he said sensibly.

Lara gave him a grateful hug. 'I knew you'd be cool.'

The doorbell went again. 'That really will be Josh,' said Bella, who had been following it all with interest.

Phoebe jumped up to follow her as she went to open the front door. 'Gib, can you get Lara a drink? I'll be back in a second.'

In the corridor, she seized Bella's arm. 'Bel, you've got to go and get everything out of Gib's room,' she whispered urgently. 'Just chuck it all in my room for now, but make it look as if his hasn't been slept in for a while. I'll keep Lara in the kitchen as long as I can.'

'Where's Gib going to sleep? Hi,' she said as she opened the door to Josh and kissed him on both cheeks. 'With you?'

'He'll have to—hi, Josh—Lara thinks we're practically engaged, and she's got to go on thinking it. Right now, I can't cope with my mother going into mourning because there's no wedding to plan!'

Josh stepped into the house. He was used to arriving in the middle of conversations like this. 'What's going on?'

'Bella will tell you,' said Phoebe with a harried look. 'I've got to get back to Lara.' She turned to head back down the corridor to the kitchen, and then thought better of it. 'Oh, Josh, if it comes up in the conversation, can you remember that Gib and I are engaged? Nothing official yet, but we're looking at rings and thinking about a date—you know the kind of thing.'

'Congratulations,' said Josh. 'I always thought you were exactly the kind of girl Gib needed!'

Phoebe looked at him uncertainly. Like Gib, it was often hard to tell whether Josh was joking or not. Either way, she decided that it would be more dignified just to ignore his comment.

She hurried back to the kitchen, where she found Lara sobbing in Gib's arms, her head burrowed into his chest while he held her comfortingly close and murmured soothingly into her blonde curls. The sight was enough to make Phoebe stop dead, her stomach wrenching with what she recognised to her horror as sheer, unadulterated jealousy, but the next instant Gib had lifted his head, and the naked appeal in his expression was enough to unknot her insides and send relief spilling through her veins instead.

'I was just trying to be nice,' he said apologetically.

Lara was overwrought by this stage, and it took some time to calm her down. She kept telling Phoebe tearfully how lucky she was to have Gib. 'Mum and Dad think he's wonderful. Mum's always boasting about him in the golf club.'

Phoebe's heart sank. Keeping up with her golfing friends was a point of pride with her mother. She would have loved telling them all about her daughter's fantastically successful fiancé. Phoebe could practically hear her. *No announcement yet, but there is a slot at the church in September, and I'm sounding out the best caterers...* She was going to be mortified when Phoebe told her that it was all over.

Oh, dear, it was all so complicated, Phoebe sighed to herself. That was the trouble with lying. There was never any end to it. All she had wanted was to make Ben's wedding easier for everyone, and now if she wasn't careful she was going to spend her entire life inventing imaginary lovers to keep her mother's end up at the golf club.

CHAPTER NINE

PHOEBE was exhausted by the end of the evening. Kate had come home with some smoked salmon that she had spotted on special offer, so they had ended up having an impromptu dinner party. Normally, sitting round the kitchen table with her friends, talking and laughing, was what Phoebe liked doing best, but the prospect of sharing a room with Gib again left her feeling edgy and she was terrified that someone would spot that beneath her discomfort lurked a drumming sense of anticipation.

Nor were matters improved by the relish with which Bella, Josh and Kate threw themselves into the pretence. Bella had rung Kate's mobile to warn her of the situation, so she played along with gusto when she got back. In fact, all three of them had an excellent time asking Phoebe and Gib awkward questions about the fictional wedding, allotting themselves key roles as bridesmaids and best man, and inventing stories to prove to Lara how in love the two of them were.

Phoebe's smile grew increasingly brittle, and the moment Lara yawned, she leapt up and offered to show her to her room. 'You must be tired,' she said eagerly, ignoring the meaningful looks the others were exchanging.

There was no sign that Gib had ever been in the spare room. Relieved, Phoebe made up the bed, kissed her sister goodnight, and made her way wearily along to her own room, where it was immediately obvious that Bella had taken her instruction to chuck Gib's stuff in there quite literally. The floor was strewn with clothes, papers, bedding and assorted bits and pieces, although his laptop had been placed—Phoebe hoped—on her bed.

Wearily, she bent to start picking things up, and she was just gathering together various papers when Gib put his head round the door. 'Can I come in?'

'This is your room now,' said Phoebe, not meeting his eyes. 'You don't need to ask.'

'Maybe I'm a very polite fiancé.' Gib came into the room, only to still as he saw that she held his passport in her hand. 'I should put that somewhere safe,' he said, and to his relief she passed it to him without insisting on looking at his photograph the way some people would.

'I'm afraid Bella was in a bit of a hurry when she cleared out your room,' she apologised. 'I hope you haven't lost anything.'

Trying desperately to remember if he had left anything incriminating out, Gib bent to help her pick up the last few papers. Fortunately he kept most of his work on his laptop, but there had been some paperwork involved with the latest project which should be here somewhere...

'Oh, here's something about the Community Bank,' said Phoebe in surprise, smoothing out a brochure on her knee. 'Where did you get this?'

'It must have been in all those papers you had,' said Gib after the tiniest of pauses. 'I probably found it when I was researching my part for the wedding.'

Phoebe studied the brochure, a slight frown between her brows. 'I don't remember this one,' she said, puzzled. 'It looks interesting, too. I'm sure I haven't seen it before.

'You had a lot of papers there. Perhaps it was caught up with everything else?'

'It must have been, I suppose.' Her shrug was baffled. 'I might as well take it back, anyway,' she decided. 'It might give me some new ideas for the programme, and it's not as if you need it any more, is it?'

'No,' said Gib. 'Of course not.'

Quickly he gathered the rest of the papers together and tidied them into a pile. 'I'll sort these out later,' he said firmly and began picking up his scattered clothes.

'I'm sorry about all this,' said Phoebe awkwardly as she handed him a shirt.

'Don't worry about it. I can see that Bella was in a hurry, and it's not as if anything's broken.'

'No, I meant about acting as my fiancé again,' she made herself explain. 'Sharing a room, all of that…you know.'

'You weren't to know Lara was going to turn up,' Gib pointed out in a reasonable voice.

'No, but I should have put a stop to the whole business ages ago,' Phoebe confessed guiltily. 'It's just that Mum's been so worried about Lara, and so thrilled at the idea that I might get married, I haven't had the heart to tell her that it's all over.'

Gib, continuing to retrieve clothing from the floor, made a non-committal sound.

'The thing is,' she struggled on, 'I don't want her to hear from Lara that we're not really a couple. She'd be devastated if she found out I had made it all up, so I wondered if…well, if you wouldn't mind getting back into your role while Lara's here?' she finished in a rush.

'No, I don't mind,' said Gib, but Phoebe, already acutely self-conscious, was convinced that his twisted smile meant that he did.

'You don't have to if you don't want to,' she said hastily.

'No, it's OK,' he said. 'I really don't mind.'

'Oh. Well…good. Thanks.'

There was an uncomfortable silence. At least, Phoebe found it uncomfortable. Gib seemed quite happy to carry on with the business of tidying up the mess Bella had created. Realising that she was just standing there, she bent to retrieve the duvet.

'It should only be for a few days,' she said as she attempted to roll it neatly, unsure whether she was trying to reassure Gib or herself. 'As soon as Lara's gone, I'll ring Mum and tell her that we've broken up.'

'I thought you were worried about disappointing her?' he said with one of his sharp blue glances.

'I am, but I suppose she's got to be disappointed some time,' sighed Phoebe. 'Otherwise we'll end up getting married for her, and then there'll be grandchildren, and before we know where we are we'll be spending our entire lives together!'

'And we can't have that, can we?' Gib murmured, but there was something in his voice that made Phoebe look at him in puzzlement.

'I can't imagine you'd want to impersonate the president of an international bank for ever! It wouldn't take long for even Mum to start wondering why someone so successful was driving around in my old car, and living in my old house which we could never afford to do up.'

'I guess that would be a bit of a give-away,' he agreed.

After another puzzled look, Phoebe turned away to start clearing a space in her wardrobe. 'Um...would you be happy with the same terms as last time?' she asked, putting his shirts onto hangers.

'You mean the same rules of engagement?' asked Gib sardonically, and her face burned.

'Those, of course, but I was thinking more about money.'

'Oh, that,' he said. 'No.'

She hadn't anticipated such a flat response. 'You want more?'

'I don't want any money, Phoebe!' For the first time, Gib

sounded really angry. 'How can you even ask me that? I thought we were friends now?'

Phoebe was taken aback. She had never seen him look so forbidding. 'We are,' she said but Gib pounced on the uncertainty in her voice.

'You don't sound very sure,' he accused her. 'You said you would miss me earlier. Did you mean it, or were you just saying it?'

She swallowed. 'Of course I meant it.'

'I'm going to miss you, too,' he said deliberately. 'I think that means we're friends, and you don't offer to pay friends for helping you out.'

To her amazement, Phoebe realised that he wasn't angry, he was hurt. 'Sorry,' she muttered.

'No, I'm sorry.' Gib was instantly contrite. 'I shouldn't have shouted at you. I hated the idea that you might not think of me as a friend after all. I guess I just...wanted you to like me,' he finished, appalled at how gauche he sounded, he who was so famous for his charm and his smooth talking.

Phoebe had been in the middle of putting one of his shirts on a hanger, but at that she paused, clutching it to her chest. She couldn't believe how unsure of himself Gib sounded. It was hard to remember now how irritated she had been by his confidence and charm.

Now all she could think about was the fact that he wanted her to like him.

There was a tight feeling in Phoebe's chest, and her breath had shortened uncomfortably. 'I do,' she said.

'You didn't like me when I arrived,' Gib accused her.

'No,' she admitted. There was no use in pretending that she had. 'I thought you were cocky. You reminded me of Slimy Seb, who was so horrible to Kate. He used to think that all he had to do was smile and everyone would fall over themselves to do whatever he wanted, which they usually

did, of course. He hurt her so badly, I didn't like the thought
that you might come in and do the same.'

She paused, trying to understand herself the point at
which her attitude towards him had changed. 'And then
you…you changed everything,' she said slowly. 'You hang
around the house, not doing anything, and half the time you
drive me nuts, while the other half I spend feeling jittery
because I don't know what you're going to do or say next,
but yes, I do like you,' she told him, as if goaded. 'I don't
really know why, but I do.'

A smile started in Gib's blue eyes and spread out, illu-
minating his face. 'I like you, too,' he said.

Taking the shirt and hanger from Phoebe's nerveless
hands, he tossed them onto the bed. 'Come here,' he said
and enfolded her in a warm hug. Almost of their own vo-
lition, her arms crept round his back to hug him back.

It felt so good to be held against him again. It felt warm
and safe and somehow right, like coming home. Phoebe
rested her face against Gib's neck and breathed in the scent
of his skin with a giddy rush of pleasure. *He liked her.*

And then the pleasure congealed in her veins as it dawned
on her that she didn't like Gib at all. It was much, much
more than that.

She loved him.

The world seemed to rock around Phoebe as the realisation seeped through her, and instinctively she clung to him
even as she stiffened in his arms, and Gib's hold tightened
in response. She felt his lips brush her hair and her heart
began to batter relentlessly, so convinced was she that he
would turn his head and kiss her.

But Gib didn't kiss her. He released her instead and
smiled down into her face. 'I like you a lot,' he told her.

Like, not love.

Phoebe stepped back, shaken by the terrifying new

knowledge that was churning around inside her. 'I don't know why,' she muttered, hugging her arms together. 'I've been horrible to you.'

'I know,' said Gib, but he was teasing her. The blue eyes were alight with laughter and one corner of his mouth curled irresistibly. 'There's no accounting for it at all!'

'Perhaps you don't really like me at all,' she said unsteadily.

There, that was his cue. Say I don't like you, Gib, she willed him mentally. Say I love you.

The smile faded from his eyes and he was suddenly serious. 'I do,' he said. 'I like your strength and your loyalty. I like your sharpness and the way you put up your chin sometimes and the bravery in your eyes. You can put up your prickles all you like, Phoebe, but I know there's a very nice person hiding in there.'

Phoebe looked away. She didn't want to be a very nice person. She was sick of being strong. She wanted Gib to think of her as warm and desirable, not just *very nice*.

He was only two steps away. More than anything, she longed to close the gap between them, to press her lips into his throat and feel his arms around her once more. She wanted him to kiss her and tell her that he wanted her the way she suddenly, desperately wanted him.

Terrified that her body would move towards him of its own accord, Phoebe made herself turn away. She picked up the shirt and hanger from the bed where Gib had thrown them. He would be aghast if she suddenly threw herself at him like that, but tonight…tonight they would be sharing a bed, and there were some things that were easier said in the dark.

She cleared her throat. 'Well, at least now we know that we like each other it should make it easier than last time. Sharing a bed, I mean.'

'Do you think so?' Gib's voice was very dry. She had been so warm and tempting in his arms. He could still feel the silkiness of her hair underneath his cheek, still smell her tantalising fragrance. 'I don't. I think I'd better sleep on the floor tonight.'

Phoebe looked at him in dismay. 'On the floor? Why?'

'Your bed is much too small for a start,' he said, nodding at where it was pushed up against a wall. 'It was hard enough last time, Phoebe,' he went on with a crooked smile, 'and you remember how big that four-poster was.' He glanced back at her bed. 'If I had to sleep with you in that, I wouldn't be able to keep my hands off you!'

The air evaporated around Phoebe. 'Would...would that be such a bad thing?' she asked breathlessly.

Gib steeled himself to stay where he was and keep his hands fixed firmly to the pillow he was holding. 'It would be for you,' he said. 'Ben's been married less than a month. I know how much he meant to you, and that you're not over him yet.'

She had told him that she was still in love with Ben, Phoebe remembered. She had let him believe it, even when she had known that it wasn't true any more. How could she tell Gib now that he was the one she loved? Even if she were to convince him that she wasn't just on the rebound from Ben, telling him would just spook him. He might like her, but he had said nothing about love.

Love implied commitment and staying and settling down. Those weren't words she associated with Gib at all. He was a free spirit, too restless and open to new experiences to want to tie himself down to one girl. Phoebe imagined a succession of beautiful blondes telling him that they loved him only to hear a casual goodbye in return. She would only be the latest in a very long line.

If only it made a difference. If only knowing that he

would be leaving soon would stop her being in love with
him, but now that she had admitted it to herself, it had taken
her over completely. Cool reason stood no chance against
the way her body ached for him. All Phoebe cared about
was being with him that night, being able to hold him and
touch him. At least then she would have something to remember.

'Maybe,' she said in a low voice, 'sleeping with you is
what I need to help me to get over Ben.'

Gib's jaw tightened. Part of him was furious at the idea
that he might be just a way of helping her to get over Ben,
but it was all he could do to keep the rest of him from
reaching for her. It was only by reminding himself that it
wasn't what Phoebe really needed that he managed to stay
where he was.

Was this what Josh had meant when he had challenged
him to be friends with a woman? Putting her needs over his
own desire? Josh believed that you couldn't mix sex and
friendship, and Gib thought he knew what he meant now.

He wanted Phoebe very badly, but it would be different
with her. It would *mean* something. Instinctively he knew
that making love to her would be important in a way it had
never been for him before, and after that there would be no
retreat. He would find himself involved, would get tangled
up in caring and commitment and all those things he had
spent his entire adult life avoiding. Gib wasn't sure that he
was ready for that.

No, far better to keep things as they were, he decided.
Phoebe was a friend, a dear friend but still just a friend, and
that was how she would stay.

'Only time will do that, Phoebe,' he said, sounding
strained. He might think that he was doing the right thing,
but it didn't make it any easier. Was it this hard for Josh
not to reach out for Bella? he wondered bleakly.

'Perhaps,' she said, and then gathered her courage as she saw her chance slipping away. She swallowed. 'But in the meantime, I might need some comfort,' she said, going as far as she dared.

Comfort? Gib set his teeth. He didn't want to be a comfort to her! He wanted more than that.

'I don't think that's a good idea,' he said with difficulty.

Phoebe moistened her lips. 'Why not?'

Yes, why not? Why not take her in his arms and draw her down onto the bed and make love to her all night?

'I don't want to lose your friendship.'

'It wouldn't have to be like that,' said Phoebe, gripping her hands together and unable to believe how forward she was being.

'I think it would,' said Gib. 'Sex and friendship don't go together.' If he said it often enough to himself, he might even believe it. 'If I slept with you, I'd lose you as a friend, and you're too important to me for me to want to do that. I'll play my part for Lara, of course, but at night I think it's better if I sleep on the floor.'

Well, she wasn't going to beg.

'Fine,' said Phoebe stiffly. 'Whatever you want.'

She hung the shirt in her wardrobe and reached for another.

'Phoebe—' Gib began, hating to see her retreat behind her prickly mask once more.

'Yes?'

He was a little daunted by her brittle smile. 'Phoebe, you do understand, don't you? Sex always ends up complicating things, and it doesn't last. Sooner or later one of you gets bored, and then you can't go back to being friends.'

'No, I'm sure you're right,' Phoebe said, proud of how cool she sounded. 'It would have been a bad idea. It would have spoiled everything.'

Everything was spoiled anyway, though, she thought dismally. Falling in love had done that. She couldn't believe how it had happened, with Gib of all people, too! He wasn't her type at all. Really, it was such a cliché, falling for good looks and charm! Phoebe had always expected herself to be more discriminating.

She tried everything to talk herself out of it. She told herself it was just a reaction to Ben getting married, that it was a purely physical attraction that would disappear as soon as Gib left, that it wasn't really *love*. It was just wanting him and needing him and feeling more vivid and alive just because he was there.

Never had Phoebe thought that she would be grateful to Celia, but her boss's increasingly manic demands at least gave her an excuse to put in long hours at the office and avoid going home to be *friends*. She didn't want to be friends. Friends wasn't enough.

Phoebe was mortified by Gib's rejection. She couldn't have made it more obvious that she wanted to sleep with him, but he clearly didn't want her.

Why should he? She studied her reflection gloomily. She was too prickly, too fierce, too intimidating. Of course Gib would prefer sweet, pretty, winsome girls who knew how to flutter their eyelashes and smile seductively, and do all the things she could never do. It was absolutely stupid for a girl like her to fall in love with a man like him. It would never work. For the umpteenth time, Phoebe told herself to stop it at once.

Only it wasn't as easy as that. Lara was still pursuing Jed to his gigs, but they tended to start later in the evening, so she was at home when Phoebe got back. That meant that Phoebe had to smile and pretend to be happy, to let Gib touch her lightly the way a lover would do, knowing all the time that at night she would lie alone in her bed, watching his lumpy outline on the floor and wishing she could crawl under the duvet with him and put her arms round him and kiss him and make him love her.

Phoebe didn't know whether to be glad or sorry that Lara was still hanging around a week later, not having had much success in persuading Jed to let her move in with him. On the one hand, it was torture having to pretend that everything was nice and normal, but at least as long as Lara was there, Gib couldn't talk about leaving.

The thought of the house without him now was unbearable, but Phoebe knew that he would go eventually. 'I'll stay as long as you need me,' he had said, talking about the situation with Lara and she had wanted to shout at him and tell him in that case he would have to stay for ever. Instead she had nodded and thanked him politely and said that she didn't think that Lara would be staying for much longer.

Love, she thought, wasn't suiting her at all. Her eyes were dull from lack of sleep, and she had lost her appetite. Kate and Bella were beginning to look at her in concern. 'Is something the matter, Phoebe?' Kate asked one day. 'You don't look well.'

Aware of Gib's suddenly narrowed stare on her, Phoebe straightened her shoulders instantly. 'I'm fine,' she insisted. 'Just a bit tired.'

'Is Celia still giving you a hard time?'

'She keeps hassling me about this bank film and how we have to have an interview with the president,' said Phoebe, clutching at the excuse. 'I hoped she'd forgotten all about it, but now the other programme is in the can, she's back to obsessing about J.G. Grieve. She's hinting that she'll bring in someone else if I don't arrange some kind of personal interview. I think I could talk her into accepting an interview with someone else, since we're obviously not going to get J.G. Grieve, but I can't get anyone at the

Community Bank to talk to me at all.' She sighed. 'I don't know what I'm going to do—unless it's start looking for another job!'

The next evening, when she came wearily into the kitchen after another frenzied day at Purple Parrot Productions, they were all waiting for her, sitting around the table and evidently bursting with anticipation.

Phoebe looked from one to the other. 'What's going on?'

'Gib's got something for you,' said Lara, beaming.

'Oh?' As always now, her heart squeezed whenever her eyes rested on him. 'What is it?'

Getting to his feet, Gib dug a business card out of his shirt pocket. Not a diamond ring or a surprise trip to Paris, then.

'Yesterday I happened to bump into a friend of friend who turns out to work for the Community Bank,' he said. 'I didn't tell you yesterday as I wasn't sure if it would work out, but I went to see him today and asked if he would speak to you. He doesn't know if he could get you an interview with J.G. Grieve, but he might have some contacts in the organisation who could help you.'

Phoebe stared down at the card in disbelief. All this time she had been desperately trying to find a contact, and Gib *just happened* to bump into someone! She knew she ought to be delighted. This was the lead that could well save her job. Before she knew that she loved Gib, she would have been thrilled, but now it was all she could do to summon a smile.

'Thank you,' she said, and then saw the others at the table looking surprised at her muted response. They were obviously expecting her to demonstrate her gratitude in a more affectionate way.

There was nothing for it but to widen her smile. 'That's

fantastic!' she tried to enthuse and kissed Gib on the cheek. That was fair enough, surely?

His arm came round her automatically, and he held her close against him, tightening his hold when she would have stepped back and turning his head so that his mouth met hers, sending an instant, intense flare of response through her.

This might be her last chance to kiss him, Phoebe thought hazily. Lara would be leaving any day now, and then he would be gone. But for now he was here, and his arm was around her and his mouth was warm and persuasive on hers. Phoebe let herself melt into him and kissed him back, un-caring of what he or anyone thought. Her arm slid around his waist to hold him closer, while her other hand, still clutching the business card, crept to his chest and twisted in his shirt as if to anchor herself against the intoxicating rush of pleasure.

When Gib lifted his head, there were tears stinging Phoebe's eyes. She blinked them away fiercely to see Lara watching her with interest, and Bella and Kate wearing iden-tically speculative expressions. Swallowing, she made her-self step away from him.

'I'll ring this guy first thing tomorrow,' she said.

'He's on his way back to the States,' said Gib quickly. 'I'd give him a couple of days—and don't forget to tell him I gave you his number.'

Lara went out soon afterwards, announcing that Jed had a gig in Hackney and that she wanted to get there early so that she could offer to help with setting up.

'Hackney's the other side of London,' Phoebe pointed out. 'How are you going to get home?'

'Don't fuss, Phoebe. I'll be fine. Anyway, I'm hoping tonight will be the night Jed and I get back together. He

mentioned something about a party later, so don't worry if
I don't come back at all.'

Phoebe was left to avoid eye contact with Gib and her
friends. She escaped to the bath and then, pleading tiredness,
straight to bed. The tiredness was real, but she couldn't sleep
for thinking about that piercingly sweet kiss and whether it
would be the last time Gib held her. If Lara moved in with
Jed, she would have no excuse but to ring her mother and
tell her that the 'engagement' was off, just as she had promised.

Much later, Gib let himself quietly into the room.
'Phoebe?' he whispered, but she squeezed her eyes shut and
pretended to be asleep, afraid he would only want to justify
the kiss and explain that it wasn't meant to spoil their friendship. After a while, Gib lay down and rolled himself in his
duvet, and Phoebe was left to another sleepless night alone
with her aching heart.

There was no sign of Lara the next morning. Jed must
have relented after all. Phoebe wanted to be glad for her
sister, but all she could think was that now there would be
no excuse for Gib not to go, and she felt leaden inside as
she walked along to the tube.

Still, when the receptionist rang through to tell her that
Lara was on the line, Phoebe forced a smile to her face as
she asked her to put her sister through. At least one of them
should be happy.

It certainly wasn't Lara. Her voice crowded with sobs,
she told Phoebe that she was going home.

'What's happened?' Phoebe demanded in concern, but
Lara was crying in earnest by that stage and it was impossible to get anything out of her. 'Where are you?' she asked
instead, and Lara managed to tell her that she was back at
the house.

'Stay there,' said Phoebe. 'I'm coming.'

'You can't go home in the middle of the morning!' Celia objected. 'You've got too much to do. You haven't got me an edit suite yet and I need you to book those lights and when are you going to email Dave about that tripod...'

Phoebe walked out on the rest of it.

She found Lara weeping miserably, face down on the bed that had once been Gib's. For once he was out. Phoebe tried to remember the last time she had come back and he hadn't been there, and couldn't think of a single occasion. The house felt oddly empty without him, and she thought bleakly that she had better get used to it.

Sitting down on the edge of the bed, she stroked her sister's hair and coaxed the whole story out of her. She was terribly afraid that something awful had happened, but it turned out that the worst hurt was to Lara's feelings. She had finally received her much-longed-for invitation to party with the group after the gig, and when she was asked back to where they were living, she was ecstatic. It was only when she got there that she realised that Jed had been annexed by an intimidatingly cool girl and that she herself was evidently intended for the least prepossessing member of the group.

'And I'd spent all my money buying them all drinks at the club so I didn't have any left to get back here,' Lara sobbed. 'I had to stay there all night fighting this guy off, and everything was so dirty it was *horrible*! And the worst thing is that Mum and Dad are going to say 'I told you so' and I gave up my course and everything and I feel such a *fool*. They're going to be furious with me!'

Privately, Phoebe thought her parents would be so glad to see Lara safely home that they would forgive her anything, but in the end she said that she would drive her back to Bristol and face them with her. Of course, her mother insisted that she spend the night rather than driving straight back—'You'd better ring Gib, dear, and let him know where you are or he'll be worried'—so she left very early the next morning and went straight to work.

She half expected Celia to sack her there and then for walking out the previous day, but there was so much to do that even her notoriously irrational boss had realised that this was not the time to lose a key member of the team. Either that or she had realised just how much Phoebe did.

By the end of the day, Phoebe was tired and frazzled and wanted nothing more than to be at home with a strong drink. But going home would mean facing Gib and keeping her promise to ring her mother and end the pretence, so she was still sitting at her desk when she remembered the contact Gib had given her at the Community Bank.

Taking out the card, she studied it. California. It was almost seven o'clock in London by then, which meant that there was a chance that Brad Petersen would be at work. She could try, anyway.

Phoebe dialled the number before she had a chance to lose her nerve and sat listening to the foreign ringing tone. The way her luck was going at the moment, there would be no one there—but no! She was through.

'Could I speak to Brad Petersen, please?' she said, reading his name from the card.

That was as far as her luck went. Brad, it appeared, was sick and wouldn't be in for another couple of days. Was there anyone else who could help?

'I'm not sure,' said Phoebe doubtfully. 'I'm calling from London, and I was given his name by somebody called John Gibson—' She broke off as the man at the other end of the phone gave a shout of recognition.

'You don't mean Gib, do you?'

'Er...yes.' She held the receiver away from her and stared at it in puzzlement. 'Do you know him?'

He laughed. 'We certainly do! How the hell is he?'

'He's fine,' she said in a frozen voice. 'I didn't realise he knew anyone other than Brad at the Community Bank.'

'I'd say he knows just about everybody,' the man said, sounding amused.

'Really? How's that?' Phoebe couldn't believe her own control. 'Does he work for the bank as well?'

'You could say that.' Yes, that was definite amusement. 'Listen, are you likely to see him soon?'

'I'm going to see him tonight, as it happens.'

'Well, say hey from all of us in Development, will you? Tell him we've all been missing him!'

'Oh, I will,' said Phoebe. 'I'll tell him *exactly* what you've said.'

Very carefully, she put the phone down. For a while she sat, just staring at it while hurt and humiliation built gradually inside her into a white-hot fury. It was surging invigoratingly along her veins by the time she got to her feet, but she was outwardly uncannily calm as she picked up her bag, put on her coat and retrieved the car from the car park where she had left it all day. Then she drove home, her knuckles white against the steering wheel.

Kate and Bella were out, Phoebe was glad to see, and Gib was alone in the kitchen. His face lit up in a way that made her heart crack when he saw her.

'Hey!'

'Hey,' she echoed, but enunciating it very clearly. 'Oh, that's from everyone in Development, by the way!'

Gib stilled. 'Development?' he repeated cautiously.

'Surely you haven't forgotten those guys, have you?' Sarcasm dripped from her voice. 'I gather they all miss *you* a lot!'

'You didn't talk to Brad Petersen,' said Gib flatly as he realised what must have happened.

'No, Brad's sick, but it turns out that wasn't a problem, because everybody knows good old Gib!' Phoebe's eyes flashed dangerously green. *'I just happened to bump into him!'* she quoted his words back to Gib furiously. 'I couldn't believe it! All this time I've been going on and on about the Community Bank and how hard it is to contact anyone there and *you*, you actually work for them! Why didn't you tell me?'

Gib sighed. 'I didn't want to get involved with the programme. It's the bank's policy not to give personal interviews and to make sure that any publicity concentrates on the projects. You told me yourself that Celia wanted to do a hatchet job on the president. Of course I wasn't going to help you do that!'

'You lied to me!' Phoebe was too hurt and angry to listen to him. 'I hate liars!'

'I didn't lie outright,' Gib tried to defend himself.

'You said you didn't have a job!'

'I never said that. *You* assumed that I didn't, but I told you myself that I was working on various projects while I was over here.'

'Community Bank projects?'

'Yes.'

Too angry to stand still, Phoebe was striding around the kitchen like some kind of caged beast. 'No wonder you thought you'd be in banking when I wanted you to pretend that you had a job! *I know, I'll say I work for the Community Bank! I'll do some research.* Oh, good idea, I said. How stupid can you get?' she demanded bitterly. 'All you had to do was promote yourself a bit, make yourself President, because why not? Phoebe's too dense to work it out! She'll never know.'

It was all so obvious when you knew the truth, she

thought savagely. Of *course* he had been able to convince everyone that he was a banker at the wedding!

'No wonder I always thought you were laughing at me! You must have had a very amusing time seeing me make an idiot of myself, all that worrying about how you'd cope at the wedding, all that scratching my head about how to contact someone at the Community Bank—what a laugh you must have had!'

'Phoebe, it wasn't like that,' Gib tried, but Phoebe was in no mood to listen to him.

'Oh, wasn't it? What was it like then, Gib? Why couldn't you just tell me if it wasn't like that?'

Gib hesitated, then mentally threw his cards on the table. Only complete honesty would help him now, he thought.

'I couldn't tell you,' he said, 'but not because I was laughing at you. It was because of a bet.'

CHAPTER TEN

'A BET?'

Stony-faced, Phoebe listened as Gib, opting for a full confession, told her what Mallory had said, and explained how he and Josh had come to make the bet.

'So that's what all this has been for, a *bet*?' she said when he had finished, her voice shaking. 'All that stuff you were spouting about friendship and how important it was to you, and all the time it was just some stupid joke!'

'No! It wasn't a joke,' Gib protested, raking his fingers through his hair in frustration. He thought he had explained all this. 'It started out as a challenge but that's not how it ended. I never expected...I hadn't counted on you.'

'Oh, I'm sure you hadn't! I must have been a big disappointment! Bella and Kate are pushovers, of course—they'll be friends with anybody—but I was a harder nut to crack, wasn't I? I've got to give it to you, though, Gib, you worked hard on me,' said Phoebe, raw with hurt. 'And I fell for it in the end.'

Her cheeks burned with humiliation as she remembered that scene in her room. 'That was very clever, the way you pushed me into admitting that I thought of you as a friend! I suppose you were taping the whole conversation so that you could prove to Josh that you'd won the bet. Look, here's Phoebe saying that she'll miss me! What more do you need?'

'Phoebe, you've got it all wrong—'

'Oh, yes, it's all falling into place now!' Phoebe thought that she had been angry when she found out that he worked for the bank, but it was nothing compared to the rage that seized her now. 'Then I nearly spoilt everything by getting too keen. That must have been a nasty moment when I wanted to sleep with you, because you couldn't have that, could you? Sex wasn't part of the bet! I don't blame you for insisting on the floor—I'd have done the same if I got ten thousand dollars for it! And I suppose that kind little gesture of putting me in touch with your ''friend'' was by way of being a consolation prize?'

'Of course it wasn't!' Gib was having trouble keeping his own temper under control by now. 'I just didn't like seeing you so tired. I wanted to help you keep your job.'

'Oh, very noble!' she jeered. 'And no doubt Brad Petersen wasn't supposed to let on that he knew you?'

'No,' he admitted. 'I wanted to keep it secret a bit longer.'

'Well, now that the cat's out of the bag, you might as well set up an interview for me,' said Phoebe, glaring at him. 'As I understand it, you've got lots of friends at the bank, so it shouldn't be too hard. It's the least you can do after the way you've used me!'

'You used me too,' said Gib angrily, losing his precarious control on his temper. 'You went on and on and *on* about your precious Ben, making it crystal clear that I was only there as substitute for him. How do you think that made me feel? I didn't sleep with you, not because of the bet, but because I knew I would only ever be second-best to him.

'Well, sorry, Phoebe,' he swept on as she opened her mouth, not giving her a chance to speak, 'but that's not enough for me. You claim that you want to live dangerously, but you don't. You want to keep things right as they are. You'd rather stay obsessed with a man you can't have than look around to see if there might be someone else for you. You'd rather work ridiculously long hours than relax and enjoy yourself, and if work's not enough of an excuse not to try something new, there's always your family!'

'Leave my family out of this!'

'Why? You never do,' Gib retorted, equally angry by now. 'They're all perfectly capable of looking after themselves, but no, Phoebe knows best! You're the one that claims not to like lying, but that's exactly what you've been doing because you think you know how everyone feels and you think it's up to you to make it all better. Well, I've got news for you, Phoebe. You can't. You need to learn to trust people to sort out their own problems.'

'You've got a nerve, lecturing me about trust when you've spent the last six weeks pretending to be my friend!'

His jaw set. 'I wasn't pretending.'

'Friends don't lie to each other—oh, sorry, you weren't lying, were you? You just omitted to fill me in on a few little details like the fact that you've been living a double life!

'Well, you can go and live your other half now,' Phoebe told him, green eyes a-glitter with tears. 'You can stay with Josh, and give him his ten thousand dollars while you're at it. You're going to have to come to terms with losing for once, Gib. Your girlfriend was quite right. You've got no idea what women really want from a man, but I can tell you it's a lot more than a bit of superficial charm and ability to lie, which is all that you've got to offer. Sorry, but you just don't have what it takes to be a friend!'

When Bella and Kate came back later that night, they found Phoebe raging around the house, close to tears and incoherent with fury.

'What do you mean, Gib's gone?' Bella demanded blankly, latching onto the only part that she could understand.

Phoebe poured out the whole story all over again, and

was outraged to discover that her friends were a lot less concerned about Gib's deception than she was. 'How can you be so calm about it?' she asked furiously. 'He lied to you, too!'

'Oh, I don't know,' said Kate, considering the matter with infuriating reasonableness. 'The worst thing he did was to make me think that he was unemployed when in fact he apparently has a perfectly good job. It's not the end of the world, is it?'

It felt like it to Phoebe. Angrily, she brushed the tears of rage from her eyes. She was *not* going to cry over Gib. That would be the final humiliation!

'What about the bet? Don't you feel like you've been used?'

'Not really,' said Bella apologetically. 'It's not like Gib was just pretending to like us. I'm sure that he did, and we liked him.' She sighed. 'It won't be the same without him!'

'Oh, I'm *so* sorry!' fumed Phoebe, offended. 'I should have been the one to leave so that the three of you could carry on being such good friends! I mean, I'm obviously being completely unreasonable to object to someone living in my house under false pretences. I can't think *why* I'd have a problem with that!' she added sarcastically.

'Can't you?'

Phoebe was taken aback by Kate's quiet question. 'What do you mean?' she said defensively.

'Oh, Phoebe, it's so obvious! You're upset because you're in love with Gib.'

'I am not!' Phoebe spluttered furiously and then faltered as she met Kate's unwavering eyes. 'Not any more, anyway,' she said.

'No?'

'How can I be in love with someone I can't trust?' she said with an edge of desperation. 'Now I don't know if anything he told me is true. I feel as if I don't know him at all.'

'You do know him, Phoebe. He's exactly the same guy he was before. You just know that there's more to him than you thought.'

'Yes, a whole life I know nothing about!'

'That's not important,' said Kate, choosing her words with care. 'What's important is that there was something special between you. It was obvious to all of us. We could see it in Gib's face when he looked at you, and in yours when you looked at him. That wasn't a lie. Gib wasn't pretending then. He was in love with you too.'

'No, he wasn't,' Phoebe gulped back the tears. 'He wouldn't even sleep with me!'

Bella rolled her eyes. 'He would have done if he hadn't really cared about you. As it was, of *course* he didn't want to be just a substitute for Ben. He never struck me as the kind of guy who'd like being second-best, and that's what you made him feel.'

'Bella's right,' said Kate, putting her arm round Phoebe's shoulders. 'I know you're hurt, but I think you should give Gib a second chance. It's rare to have the kind of connection you had with him, and it would be a shame to throw it away without even trying to see if you could make things right.'

'I don't know how,' Phoebe confessed miserably.

'There's no point in doing anything while you're in this state,' Kate said, and even in the depths of her despair Phoebe couldn't help being amused by the reversal of their usual roles. Normally Kate was the one in floods of tears over her love life, while Phoebe stuck to being sensible. Bella was good on sympathy, but Phoebe was the one they both turned to for comfort and practical advice. All that was changed now!

'Leave it a few days until you calm down,' Bella added.

'I'm sure Gib will ring before then anyway, and if he does, give him a chance and listen to what he's got to say.'

But Gib didn't ring.

Phoebe spent the next week lurching between bitterness and despair. One minute she was furious with him for not getting in touch, the next she missed him so acutely it was like a physical pain.

She tried telling herself that any relationship would have been doomed anyway. It could never have worked. Gib had made it clear that he wouldn't be staying in London long. Presumably he would have to go back to his job at some point. It couldn't be a very important one if he had been able to spend nearly two months hanging around in London. Whatever he said about the projects he had been setting up, he had hardly been in a frenzy of activity that a top executive would have generated. Perhaps he had taken unpaid leave so that he could take up Josh's challenge. It was exactly the sort of thing Gib *would* do.

Whenever Phoebe thought about that bet, her guts twisted painfully with the memory of that conversation in her room. 'Your friendship is important to me,' Gib had said. Had that been a lie too, and if it wasn't, why, *why*, hadn't he been in touch? It didn't matter how much she hated him for using her to win his bet, all she wanted was to hear his voice.

The silence of the phone mocked her. Soon she was as bad as Kate, constantly ringing 1471 to see if anyone had called and not left a message, and checking her email obsessively, but there was nothing from Gib.

Her only glimmer of hope was a message from the Community Bank responding to their long-standing request for an interview. The head of Development would be available after all to talk about the history of the bank and the projects in which it invested. Celia bitched about not getting the president, but it was a huge coup.

Phoebe could only think that Gib had pulled some strings for her. He might not have a particularly responsible job, but she knew to her cost how charming and persuasive he could be and, judging by the phone call she had made, he had plenty of contacts in Development.

However it had happened, she wanted to believe that he had done it for her, and it gave her the excuse she needed to call him. She could thank him for his help without sounding as if she was desperate to talk to him, couldn't she?

'I'm sorry, Phoebe,' said Josh when she rang. 'He's gone.'

'Gone? Gone where?'

'Back to the States.'

'Oh.'

Phoebe almost staggered beneath the wash of desolation. Gib had gone, and he hadn't even bothered to say goodbye. With a huge effort, she swallowed the tears in her throat. 'The thing is, I think he might have helped to arrange an interview for me,' she said unsteadily. 'I just wanted to tell him that I appreciated it.' Stumbling over her words, she asked Josh if he could give her a contact number or an email address.

'I can't give it to you, I'm afraid.' Josh sounded acutely uncomfortable. 'Gib was very angry when he left. He made me promise that I wouldn't.'

So that was it.

Bella and Kate were wrong. Gib didn't love her, and he didn't want to hear from her. Wearily, Phoebe put down the phone. Her heart felt as if it had been crushed into a small, cold stone in her chest. She would survive, she knew that. She had survived Ben's rejection, and she would survive without Gib, but never had life seemed so bleak or the future so empty.

She lost all interest in her job. Even the fact that she had

arranged an interview at last seemed a hollow victory, not
that Celia gave her much credit for it, although even she
had to accept that it was more than anyone else had been
able to get.

Ten days later, the two of them flew to California with a
cameraman. It should have been a thrilling experience for
Phoebe, the high point of her career in television that far,
but all she could think about was Gib and the dull, persistent
ache in her heart.

The headquarters of the Community Bank was a light,
airy building, all wood and windows and the last word in
technology, set in beautiful grounds far from the smog and
bustle of the city. Phoebe was desperately nervous. She presumed that Gib had come back, and she didn't know
whether she longed to bump into him or dreaded it.

At the very least she might meet someone who would be
able to give him a message, she told herself, but even if she
did, what would it say? The only thing she could think of
to tell him was that she loved him and missed him and that
all she wanted was to see him again, but how could she ask
anyone to pass *that* on?

Dave, the cameraman, raved about the setting, and they
had to hang around for ages while he shot the exterior before
at last persuading him inside.

'Phoebe Lane?' They were met by a pleasant-looking
man who held out his hand with a warm smile. 'I'm Brad
Petersen. I'm *very* pleased to meet you!'

Phoebe was a little surprised at the warmth of his welcome, but she reminded herself that Americans were notoriously friendly. So this was Brad, she thought, studying him
surreptitiously as she shook his hand. He was the contact
who had been sick when she had phoned, and she wondered
how different things would have been if he had been there
and had kept Gib's secret for him.

She longed to ask if he had seen Gib, but her tongue seemed stuck to the roof of her mouth and, in any case, Celia was there looking impatient at all the attention Phoebe was getting and pushing forward to introduce herself as producer and director so that Brad knew exactly who was in charge.

Brad shook hands civilly enough, but apparently didn't understand Phoebe's lack of status, turning back to her immediately and asking her if she had had a good trip and urging her to let him know if there was anything that he could do for her.

'Thank you, no,' said Phoebe, with a nervous look in Celia's direction. 'We're just very grateful to you for agreeing to be interviewed.'

'Oh, I should have mentioned,' said Brad. 'I can't make this afternoon. A meeting that I can't miss, I'm afraid.'

'That's absolutely typical of you, Phoebe!' Celia exploded, already irritated by being effectively ignored. 'You were supposed to confirm all of this! What on earth is the point of us coming all the way out here if we're not even going to get any interview? If you'd done your job properly, we could have sorted this out before we left London and arranged a different date. As it is the whole trip is going to turn out to be a complete waste of time and money thanks to you!'

Brad shot her a look of dislike before carrying on talking to Phoebe as if Celia hadn't spoken. 'However, the president is available this afternoon, and he wondered if you'd like to interview him instead.'

Their jaws dropped in unison. 'The *president*?' said Phoebe blankly. 'Not J.G. Grieve, the president?'

'Yes.'

'But…I thought he didn't give interviews!'

Brad smiled. 'He doesn't normally, but he's prepared to make an exception in your case.'

Phoebe thought that she would long treasure the expression on Celia's face at that moment. For once even she had nothing to say.

Hardly able to believe their luck, they followed Brad through spacious open-plan offices with views out over the spectacular grounds. To Phoebe, it didn't feel like a bank at all. Everyone was smiling and relaxed, and they were all dressed very casually. With a pang, she remembered how Gib had pretended to be the president at Ben's wedding.

'Mine's a different kind of bank where you don't have to dress like a dummy all day,' he had told her and she had rolled her eyes in disbelief. How was she to have known that he was describing a real place?

Forcing down the memory, she smiled at Brad as he stepped aside to usher her into a private office. A man rather more smartly dressed than the others was sitting behind a desk, but he got up to shake hands when they appeared.

'Thank you so much for agreeing to see us, Mr Grieve,' said Phoebe politely, and he grinned.

'I'm not Mr Grieve, I'm afraid. I'm just his assistant, but he is expecting you.'

He knocked on a door behind him, and opened it in response to a muffled 'come in' from inside. 'The film crew from London are here,' he said and held open the door so that they could file past him.

They found themselves in a vast office with glass walls on two sides and a polished wooden floor. The desk was bare except for a computer and a telephone, and two cream sofas faced each other over a low glass table. A man was lounging on one of them, but he laid the report he was reading aside and stood up as they came in.

'Welcome to the Community Bank,' he said, and smiled.

A very familiar smile.

It was Gib.

Phoebe stopped dead so that Celia, following close on her heels, bumped into her.

'Do look where you're going, Phoebe,' she snapped and pushed past her to shake Gib's hand and introduce herself.

She ignored Phoebe, who stood as if riveted to the spot. It was as if the floor was shifting dangerously beneath her feet, and she didn't dare move in case she fell over.

There was a roaring in her ears and she swallowed convulsively to wake herself up, because clearly she had fallen asleep on the plane and this was just a dream—a nightmare!—where everyone else was treating a surreal situation as completely normal. Any minute now a flight assistant would prod her to ask if she wanted a meal, and she would wake up with a start.

'Where do you want Mr Grieve sitting?' Celia asked Dave, and they started conferring about light and angles, while Gib strolled over to where Phoebe still stood by the door.

'Hello, Phoebe,' he said softly.

'You're not the president of this bank,' said Phoebe very carefully, to show that she knew this was a dream.

'I'm not?' Gib looked down at himself in mock dismay. 'Well, don't tell anyone else! They all think that I am, and we don't want them to know I've just been pretending all this time!'

For a dream, this was going on a little too long, and Gib himself was uncannily real.

And achingly familiar. The laughter lines creasing his face. The devilry dancing in the blue eyes. The shape of his jaw and the line of his throat and the way the long, mobile mouth curled into that smile that cracked her heart.

Phoebe moistened her lips, not sure now whether she

wanted it to be a dream or not. 'You can't be,' she said hoarsely.

Gib went over to the door and called for his assistant. 'Mark, am I president of this bank?'

'Er…yes, sir.'

'There you go,' said Gib, turning back to Phoebe. 'Mark says I am, so I must be.'

This couldn't be happening! 'So who is J.G. Grieve?' she managed to ask. 'Or was your name another lie?'

'J for John and G for Gibson, I'm afraid, Phoebe.'

'Phoebe!' Celia was snapping her fingers irritably. 'Don't just stand there! Dave needs you to sort out the cables and get the boom organised.' Pasting a smile on her face, she turned to Gib. 'Mr Grieve, if you'd like to sit down over there, I'll run through the questions I'd like to ask you while they're setting up.'

Numbly, Phoebe moved cables around and tested for sound, oblivious to Dave's curious looks. When he judged they were ready, Celia started on the interview. She might be a prima donna of the first order, but she could switch on the professionalism when it counted.

Not that Phoebe took in any of it. She couldn't take her eyes off Gib. She saw him talking, smiling, looked relaxed in front of the camera, but his words were drowned out by the hammering of her heart and the whirl in her head where disbelief jostled with humiliation at this final deception, but neither was as strong as the sheer joy beating along her veins, telling her that this was real after all and that he was there, he was there, he was there!

Celia was winding up. 'Why did you decide to break with precedent and talk to us this afternoon?' she asked at last.

Gib took his time before replying. He seemed to be picking his words carefully, and Phoebe found herself leaning forward to hear what he had to say.

'I've always believed that what we do here is not about us, but about the projects around the world that we support. But support is the keyword. The people who are really making a difference are those who set up the projects and devote their time and energy to making them a success. I used to think that by giving interviews that focus on me or the Community Bank, we would divert attention away from what really matters, which are the communities who are working to improve their own lives.'

'So what made you change your mind?' asked Celia.

He looked directly at Phoebe, who was holding the boom out of camera shot. 'I spent some time away from the bank recently,' he said, 'and I realised that believing something doesn't always make it true. I know now that it's not a sign of weakness to change your mind, or to admit that you were wrong.'

His eyes held Phoebe's and she looked back at him, knowing that he wasn't talking about giving media interviews any more. 'I was wrong about a lot of things,' he went on. 'Doing this interview was the only way I could think of to put things right.'

'Ah,' said Celia, evidently baffled. She exchanged a glance with the cameraman, who shrugged.

'I hoped that it would be a chance to explain,' said Gib without taking his gaze from Phoebe. 'I had something very special, and I didn't realise what it meant to me until I had thrown it away. I wanted a chance to say that I was sorry, and that I didn't understand until too late that my life had changed without me knowing it.'

'Er...right. Well, thanks very much,' said Celia, having obviously decided that Gib had lost it completely. 'Have you got all the shots you need, Dave?'

The cameraman, more perceptive, was looking at Phoebe.

'For now,' he said, and gently took the boom from her nerveless hand. 'I'll take this, love.'

Phoebe couldn't move. She could just look back at Gib, while Dave deftly packed up the kit and propelled a confused Celia out of the office. The door closed on her demand to know what on earth was going on, and why Phoebe was just *standing* there like an idiot...

Gib got up from the sofa, but he made no move to touch Phoebe. 'I hurt you,' he said. 'I'm sorry.'

'Josh said you were angry,' she found her voice at last.

'I was, but mostly with myself. I'd been selfish and arrogant and stupid, and all the things I swore I never wanted to be. I hadn't thought about you or how you might feel when you found out that I wasn't who you thought I was.'

He paused. 'I should have told you, Phoebe. I know that now. The bet wasn't important, but there never seemed to be a good moment, and I was afraid that if I did tell you it would spoil everything—which it did when you found out anyway.

'So of course I found excuses for myself,' he said. 'I told myself that I didn't mean anything to you, that I was a free spirit and that the last thing I wanted was to tie myself down. I was the guy who ran a mile at the first hint of commitment. Why would I want to give up my freedom for a girl who wasn't even in love with me? A girl who as far as I could see didn't even like me?'

'But I told you I liked you,' said Phoebe.

'I know, but you didn't sound very sure.'

'Well, I suppose that's because I wasn't. I'm afraid that I was lying too. I didn't like you.'

Gib's face fell ludicrously. 'You said that you did!'

'I didn't mean it,' said Phoebe, shaking her head sorrowfully, but the expression in the blue eyes made her stop teasing then. 'I do much more than like you, Gib,' she told him softly. 'The truth is that I love you.'

He stared at her for a long moment and then reached out to take both her hands. 'You love me?'

'Yes.' It was a release to say it at last. 'I was just too scared to admit it.'

'You love me,' he said again, trying out the words with a different intonation as if he couldn't take them in.

A smile wavered on Phoebe's lips. 'Yes.'

'Phoebe...' Gib drew her closer. 'Say it again.'

'I love you.'

'And I love you.' Gib let go of her hands to cup Phoebe's face, and she thought that she would dissolve with happiness at the warmth in the blue eyes. 'I never thought that I would say that, but it's true. You must believe me.'

'I do,' she said, and he kissed her then.

Phoebe melted into him, winding her arms around Gib's neck as the grey misery that had settled in her since he left was washed away in a tumbling tide of happiness and relief. Adrift in enchantment, she clung to him and kissed him back, again and again, deep, sweet, hungry kisses that said more than words could ever do.

'I've been so unhappy without you,' she mumbled, pressing kisses into his throat. It was much later by then, and she was sitting on his lap on one of the cream sofas. 'Why didn't you tell me you loved me?'

'Sheer jealousy,' Gib confessed, stroking her hair. 'You kept telling me that you were still in love with Ben, and I thought I would only ever be second-best for you. I tried telling myself that I would forget you quickly enough when I came back here, but I didn't. I missed you.' His arms tightened around her. 'I missed you more than I can say. I've always had a great life here. I've got everything I need—a fantastic job, a great house, wonderful friends—but none of them meant anything without you.

'And I felt guilty, too, about the way I had hurt you. I remembered what you'd said about making myself useful, and I decided that you were right. The least I could do for you was to let you have the interview you needed, and to hell with policy as long as you kept your job.'

'I wondered if it was you that had arranged it,' said Phoebe, snuggling closer. 'But I imagined you pulling strings with your superiors, not being the one who made the decision! I thought we were coming to interview Brad Petersen, though.'

'I asked Brad to do it at first because I was still feeling raw, but when it came down to it, I couldn't bear the idea that you might be in the building and I wouldn't see you. As soon as you walked in here, I knew it was hopeless,' said Gib. 'It wasn't enough just to apologise and retire with my pride intact. I knew that I had to tell you that I loved you.

'You know, Josh was right,' he went on thoughtfully. 'He told me that I was spoilt, and I was. I was bored with girls falling in love with me, and then going off in a huff when I didn't fall in love back. I never had to make an effort for any of them…and then I met you. The one person I wanted, the one person it seemed I couldn't have.'

Phoebe sat back in his lap and looked at him seriously. 'Gib, are you sure I'm not just another challenge for you, like climbing a mountain?'

'Climbing isn't a challenge,' Gib protested, pretending outrage. 'It's a passion! That feeling when you get to the summit and look out over the world…it's incredible, and it's the only thing that even comes close to the feeling I got when you told me you loved me just now.'

He smiled as his warm hand slid seductively up her thigh.

'And I have a feeling,' he said, dropping his voice until it was so deep and so low that it vibrated up and down Phoebe's spine, making her shiver with delicious anticipation, 'that the feeling I got then is only a fraction of what I'm going to feel when I finally take you to bed!'

'Are you sure you wouldn't rather stay just good friends?' asked Phoebe provocatively, even as her own hands were drifting teasingly over his body. 'Sex and friendship don't go together, you said. It just complicates things, you said. It would spoil everything.'

'Ah, yes, but that was when I thought a friend was all you'd ever be,' said Gib. 'Friendship is all very well, but when you're in love, it isn't enough. I need more from you than that. I need to know that you love me, that you will always be there, that I'll see you every morning when I wake up...and sex goes very well with all of that!'

Phoebe smiled. 'I suppose we could always try it and see,' she suggested, and Gib flipped her expertly beneath him and slid down until they were both lying horizontally on the sofa.

'We could,' he agreed, kissing his way along her jaw, 'but I think we should agree a few rules of engagement first.'

'Engagement as in battle?' she teased, breathless beneath the blizzard of kisses.

'Engagement as in getting married and living happily ever after,' said Gib into the curve of her neck so that she stretched and shivered with pleasure.

'What exactly is involved in these rules?'

'Oh, they're easy,' he murmured, continuing his delicious assault. 'First of all, you have to love me for ever.'

'I think I can manage that,' said Phoebe, not without difficulty as his lips drifted onwards.

'You might have to prove it by kissing me on a regular basis.'

She pretended to sigh. 'If I must.'

'And when we do kiss,' said Gib, 'we don't want any misunderstandings. It means everything.'

'Like this?'

Phoebe pulled him close and they kissed, a long, long kiss of promise with an undertow of dizzy, intoxicating desire.

'Exactly like that,' Gib managed raggedly at last.

'So what's the second rule?'

'I thought you'd guess this one,' he said. 'Stick to the story and keep it simple!'

She stretched luxuriously beneath his increasingly insistent hands. 'What is the story this time?'

'The same as it was before,' said Gib. 'We met, we fell in love, and we're going to spend the rest of our lives together. The only difference is that this time it's true. Do you think you can remember that?'

'Oh, I think so,' she said.

'No deviating from the script now!' he warned. 'That's the rule. You have to promise to marry me or the deal is off.'

'It doesn't sound *too* hard,' she allowed, smiling.

'I wanted to keep them simple so you know exactly what you're agreeing to,' said Gib.

'Hhmmn.' Phoebe pretended to consider.

'Just two rules,' he said. 'Love me for ever and marry me soon—what could be easier than that? It's up to you whether you accept them or not, but once you do, I have to tell you that they're not negotiable. Oh, that's the third rule!'

'In that case,' said Phoebe with a sigh of contentment, 'I accept.'

'All the rules?' said Gib, just to make sure.

'Every one of them!'

Harlequin Romance®

is delighted to present a brand-new miniseries
that dares to be different...

TANGO

FRESH AND FLIRTY...
IT TAKES TWO TO TANGO

Exuberant, exciting...emotionally exhilarating!

These cutting-edge, highly contemporary stories
capture how women in the twenty-first century
really feel about meeting Mr. Right!

Don't miss:

July:
MANHATTAN MERGER
—by international bestselling
author Rebecca Winters (#3755)

October:
THE BABY BONDING
—by rising star
Caroline Anderson (#3769)

November:
THEIR ACCIDENTAL BABY
—by fresh new talent
Hannah Bernard (#3774)

And watch for more
TANGO books to come!

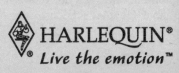

HARLEQUIN®
Live the emotion™

Visit us at www.eHarlequin.com   HRTANGJ3

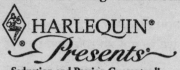

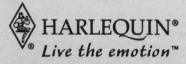

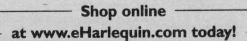

BETTY NEELS

*Harlequin Romance® is proud to present this
delightful story by Betty Neels. This wonderful novel is
the climax of a unique career that saw Betty Neels
become an international bestselling author, loved by
millions of readers around the world.*

A GOOD WIFE
(#3758)

*Ivo van Doelen knew what he wanted—he simply needed to
allow Serena Lightfoot time to come to the same conclusion.
Now all he had to do was persuade Serena to accept
his convenient proposal of marriage without her
realizing he was already in love with her!*

**Don't miss this wonderful novel—
brought to you by
Harlequin Romance®!**

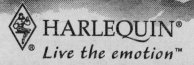

HARLEQUIN®
Live the emotion™

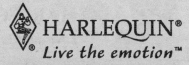

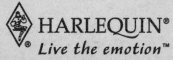